THE TALISMAN

THE TALISMAN

CECILY CROWE

THORNDIKE PRESS • THORNDIKE, MAINE

Library of Congress Cataloging-in-Publication Data
Crowe, Cecily.
  The talisman.

  Large print edition.
  1. Large type books. I. Title.
[PS3553.R59T35 1987]   813'.954   87-1878
ISBN 0-89621-793-0 (alk. paper)

Large Print edition available in North America by arrangement
with St. Martin's Press, Inc.

Cover design by Bernie Beckman.

THE TALISMAN

CHAPTER 1

I. . . .

From my window I watch Munro, the hall porter, aided by Severn, "the lad," as they dispatch the shooting parties. Dougal the gamekeeper supervises, and the men in drab all-weather gear assembled around the Land Rovers mutely await his word. In the pale light of early morning they are like commandos setting out on a raid. They'll return in the late afternoon exhausted, staring, full of the mystique of comradeship under fire. But they are only grouse hunters, mainly English, and they'll spread their withered trophies on the small courtyard lawn to be photographed. Is there anything deader-looking than dead birds?

Next I hop quite nimbly, and quietly, so as not to wake Dottie O. next door, across my bedroom to the windows overlooking the loch. The man-of-all-work, who busies himself about the place and whose name I don't yet know, is seated in a little boat far out on the glossy lead-colored water, catching fish for the few women like myself and my sister-in-law and Dottie O. who do not shoot and take lunch at the castle. The man has blond whiskers and wears kilts, and he sits motionless, hunched over, as if nursing a grudge. The hills lift all around him like the walls of a fjord, silver-green in the mists and breathing out a heavy fragrance of wet grass and wet sheep and somber northern wildness. Munro, the ever-helpful hall porter, ever ready to contribute to the wild other-world atmosphere, says the loch, is as deep as it is wide.

"Bottomless, Munro?"

"Och, aye, mistress, bottomless." Even *och, aye* has a raw portentous sound. "And cold as a tomb."

I respond as if to an omen, with a little shiver.

That's what there is to see at dawn.

And strangely stirring, I find. I don't know what I expected to feel. I wouldn't have been surprised to feel sadness. But hopping from window to window at dawn, writing at my desk late at night, I am filled for the first time in months with energy, something like a private excitement, as if this remote place were a threshold, the result of an as yet incalculable cast of fortune's dice.

Can this be merely the effect of Bart's ancestral country? Or is it the result of *change*, recommended by Dr. Kohl, change from confinement in hospital and home for so many months, when I was unable even to hop? Or is it a new-begotten appreciation of life in general?

Even my face, as I pass a mirror, looks different.

The expression is large-eyed and hopeful, the dark hair starting away from the white brow (on which the plastic surgeon did such a perfect job), the wrenched expression of one who has been thrust forward, and has squeaked by, the gates of hell. Come to think of it, I had this wide-eyed hopeful expression before the accident as well as after. Bart used to say, "Honey, sometimes you look nine instead of twenty-nine."

But now there's a faint rose color in the cheek bones and a shine on the skin. The circles under the eyes have faded. The breasts have filled out again, and the spindly thighs; flesh has covered the grotesquely protruding hipbones.

The fact is, as Dr. Kohl must have guessed, there are no reminders of Bart here, for Bart never set foot in Scotland. His ancestors were Scots but he himself never came here. There is no Bart-vacuum. His death doesn't get between us, and I'm free to remember him alive. And how alive, how all-prevalent, he was! (As for the baby, it's as if it never had life at all, even in my womb. Unborn, unformed, it bled away from me in a hospital room and I can't even remember my prenatal dreams for it. The vacuum left by my great grand Bart took up all available emotional space, sucked in all possible anguish.) It's ten months since the accident and Bart's death, but now in this unlikely land he seems closer to me.

It may have been plain to everyone, particularly to Lilah, my sister-in-law, that I chose to come here for Bart's sake, making a pilgrimage he was never able to find time for, fulfilling his promise.

"Would you believe," he told me, "I'm a landowner in Scotland?" The very name of the country had an unreal sound to us, lying in the California sun, newly married and still getting to know each other. "Some old impoverished laird had to sell off land, and my Scots grandfather, having made his pile in the States, picked it up. He had his eye on the castle, too, no doubt to set himself up as the local boy who made good, like Andrew Carnegie, but somehow the old laird managed to hang onto it. Or so my father told me. Anyway the land is mine now and I've never seen it. A few hundred acres, as I recall. I don't think my father ever visited it either."

Bart seldom had twinges of conscience, but

even with his multitude of concerns and responsibilities he must have had misgivings about this faraway patch of Scotland, snatched up long ago from a hard-pressed nobleman and abandoned to the elements ever since. "Doesn't seem right, does it, to own land and never bother to look at it? We'll make a side trip some day, Sue, when we're stopping in London, and fly up."

In his will Bart stipulated the land was to be returned to the Strathburne family on my death, leaving me the option of enjoying it myself.

So here I am, without him, making his pilgrimage for him, and oddly, unforseeably, exhilarated. We arrived last week – Lilah, Dottie O., and I – and already my blood pressure is nearer normal. (My blood pressure needs coaxing up, not down.) "You were right and I was wrong," Dottie confessed, pocketing her sphygmo-gismo. "This trip is doing you *good*."

"My blood is sitting up and taking notice," I told her. "After all, there's a bit of Scots in my background, too."

II. . . .

Next, after checking out whatever is going on below my windows, I start my exercises, ma-

11

neuvering myself to the floor by way of the knobs on an incredible mahogany armchair, like a mad wood-carver's entry in a contest for Queen Victoria's throne. I grit my teeth. But no tears, now. The challenge outweighs pain — the new energy, the new freedom, the sense of threshold!

Dottie O. came in this morning in the middle of the ritual. "By Jesus, girl, you're gonna make it!" She doesn't wear her uniform here, and her tall robust figure in ordinary dress is something to behold. She looks, as Bart would have said, like a description of a missing person. Today she wore a green and purple tartan skirt, bought on the drive up from Glasgow, a red turtleneck shirt under a yellow cardigan, and white rubber-soled shoes. She squatted down beside me. "That's it, now, stre-e-etch. Little farther, little farther. Hey, great! See? Sue-baby, you're getting there. Once more, now, for Dottie."

Time was when I gritted my teeth not only to contain pain but to contain fury at Dottie O'Halloran. "Sadist!" I croaked at her, weeping. But never did I nor ever will I forget her tough loving-kindness throughout the endless lurid hospital nights, and later at home on the hilltop in Montecito when I was trying to give up the painkillers and sedatives, and Dottie, kneading my spasm-wracked flesh as casually as if she were making bread, reeled off one joke after another, most of them dirty. I laughed and cried at the same time.

Lilah wandered in, in her nightgown, one of those rough nights, for she was staying in the house with me, a staunch sister-in-law I'd never properly valued before. "Oh, Dottie," she cried, "must she go through this? Can't you see she's in agony? Give her her pill, for God's sake!"

Dottie turned to her, making a common slip in the heat of the moment. "Listen, Mrs. Malarkey!"

Lilah's brows shot up. "Mrs. *Mac*-Larkie, if you please." All three MacLarkie brothers, Bart told me, had had to endure this slip once in a while, especially as schoolboys, but Bart, the oldest, was a strapping black-haired fellow even as a youngster and had only to issue a quiet warning to put a stop to it.

"Mrs. *Mac*-Larkie," Dottie echoed irritably. "And let's get this straight, too, if you please: I take my orders from Dr. Kohl. He says it's time to taper off the medication. Do you want Susan to kick the habit or don't you?"

Poor Lilah quailed, and fled.

"I guess all nurses who'd been on a case a long time become bossy," sniffed Lilah, the next day. She'd proved herself to be a regular lion of strength in the past months, but she likes to

13

play the role of mouse. Only her sense of humor gives her away. "*And* cranky." She gave me her droll glance. "But I asked for it, so I guess it's my own fault."

"Fault, Lilah?" I often find myself rising to Lilah's own defense. For it was Lilah who saw a way to get me out of the hospital sooner by prevailing on Dottie to come home with me. "I have you to thank for it! We couldn't have managed without her."

I have much more to thank Lilah for. She has stood by me unfailingly since the accident. Again and again I came to, when I was out of Intensive Care, to find Lilah's small plump comforting figure beside my hospital bed, the ceiling light shining on her fine blond hair. And later, when I was well enough to be told what had happened, she held my hand in compassionate silence. She, too, had gone through the shock of widowhood. Andrew MacLarkie had died of a heart attack the year before I met Bart.

So I kicked the habit, and eventually I reached the plateau of recovery that made Dr. Kohl feel I needed a change.

Lilah disapproved of the Scotland idea. "I do understand your curiosity about the property, dear." We were on the pool terrace, Lilah needlepointing under an umbrella (she was doing a whole set of dining-room chairs for me), and I, seated on the pool's edge nearby, gently scissoring my legs in the water. Scissoring was part of my therapy, although it wasn't safe yet to swim. Below us the view of descending hills shimmered in the afternoon heat. "But, Susan, you'll have plenty of time in the future for a long trip like that. Shouldn't you at least wait until you can walk without a crutch? Surely it's too soon!"

"I have Dr. Kohl's permission if I take Dottie O. with me."

"*Dottie?*" That seemed to set her back. "Would she go?"

"She said, By Jesus she would."

True, Dottie did say it, but only after a long wrangle. She didn't like the idea of Scotland any better than Lilah. Scotland was gloomy, wasn't it? The prospect gave her bad vibes. And what would she do about Sam? (Sam is her policeman-husband.) I said Sam was used to fetching for himself when she was on a case; couldn't he spare her for a few weeks? I said, You'd go like a shot if it was Ireland, wouldn't you? I said, Do I have to hire a strange nurse to go with me? I beat her down, for once.

"But, Susan," Lilah persisted as we sat by the pool, "do you know anyone who's stayed at this castle? In September? It might be damp and cold. Does it have central heating? Private baths? An elevator? It sounds as if you'd picked the most uncomfortable place in all of Europe. Oh, Susan, I'd worry so about you!"

"Then come with us."

I could all but hear Bart say, "There you go again." My waifs-and-strays complex, he called it. "Susan-honey," said Bart, ruffling my hair — and he only mussed my hair when I was being particularly foolish — "you can't *make* people happy!" I had to laugh, realizing how much naive egotism lay behind my charitable impulses. Bart's good nature never conflicted with his level-headedness. Yet obviously I wasn't cured.

"Susan!" Lilah laid aside her needlework and her mild gray-blue eyes stared down at me. "You're not serious."

"Of course I'm serious," I blustered, as though defending myself to Bart. "The change would be good for you, too, Lilah. Unless you need a change from *me*, and I would certainly understand that."

"Oh no, dear, but —" Lilah considered, and I knew she was tempted, although she twisted her entwined fingers together as she does when she's troubled or confused.

"You're trying to think of reasons why not," I

told her. "Look, I'd worry about *you*, alone again in your apartment. You know money is no object. It's not only my treat, Lilah, it's my privilege." Talk about egotism! "Come with us, if only to see that we *are* comfortable, and if you don't care for it yourself you can leave us whenever you like. We'll have a week in New York first, for shopping and the theater. Oh, come, Lilah — I'd miss you!" And I meant it, sincerely. I'd miss her quiet dependable presence, always nearby, gently unobtrusive but aware, her flashes of comedy.

"Would you, dear?" Her eyes looked ready to fill with tears. "Would you really miss me?" And then the little telltale lines of humor appeared at the corners of her mouth. "Dumpy little me?"

I have to throw back my head and laugh when she pulls this sort of thing, just saving herself from bathos. I have to hug her if she's within reach. And I couldn't help wondering, in light of Bart's level-headedness, if the accident and my being so badly incapacitated had done something for Lilah, had given her a chance to be needed, to contribute something of herself. Even when her husband Andrew was alive she may have been overshadowed, for according to Colin, the youngest and now the sole surviving brother, all the MacLarkies had a tendency to

17

come on strong. (A bachelor, and not to be compared in terms of virility with Bart, or probably Andrew, Colin is nevertheless another charmer.) I, too, let's face it, was overshadowed by Bart, but content to be — grateful to be!

In the end Lilah, also, was persuaded to come to Scotland.

And so far it's working out well enough. There is no love lost between Lilah and Dottie but we manage to get along together. Lilah naps a lot and does her tapestry-work and has left off wringing her hands. Dottie O'Halloran runs riot with tartans. My blood presses upward. The castle, still owned by a descendant of the old laird although turned into a hotel, is quite comfortable. There is no elevator but the main staircase is wide and the steps shallow, and I can negotiate them with Dottie's help. There are a few newly installed private baths, and the frugal central heating is supplemented by hearth fires. The staff is small but eager to please. There are fresh flowers everywhere.

Too quiet for some tastes, no doubt, especially during the day when the grouse hunters are off on the moors, and late at night when the silence is so intense it's like a kind of alertness. One hears in this silence the resonance of the past. Strathburne Castle was built in the thirteenth century as a fortress against marauding clans, and there is an animate quality in its midnight stillness as if its history, once set in motion, had never found rest.

Quiet or not, gloomy or not, I take to it.

And another thing, a personal serendipity, though a poor substitute for Bart: here I can write again. I follow my erstwhile advice to would-be writers: start by keeping a journal. Editor of Bart's company newsletter – that's how our paths crossed in the first place – I moonlighted in my spare time by writing short stories. (Singularly inconsequential, they seem to me now as if written by another person.) Bart asked me once, finding me idle by the pool, "Honey, why don't you write any more?"

I answered, after a moment's thought, "Because I don't need to."

I meant that life with Bart was too buoyantly fulfilling, and I think my answer pleased him. It was the truth but I wonder if it was the whole truth. Bart thought for me and planned for me and I wanted for nothing. Did being overshadowed mean being lazy? The fact is, I didn't have the energy, the energy generated by aloneness, which I've rediscovered here.

I put an end to such thoughts. Why look too closely? I have more than enough aloneness now.

CHAPTER 2

I. . . .

This morning the sun came out for the first time since we arrived, and I had a sense of everything shifting at last into high gear, as if a go-ahead signal had flashed on. I'd had a long convalescence and I was at last ready. (Ready for what, I demurred, conditioned to shrink from any possibility of pain. Was there indeed something ill-omened in my coming here?) But the day was too brilliant, too beautiful, for misgivings; my new energy took charge. I dressed in a wool suit, the violet one, to go outdoors, unaided except for my crutch.

Dottie accompanied me down the staircase and left me to venture on my own. She's on hand when I need her, for exercises, for climbing in and out of the tub, for stairs, but she knows the more I can do for myself the better.

"Lilah's in the garden," she told me, not, I guessed, in case I wanted to join her, but in case I didn't want to.

I smiled noncommittally. "Okay, Dottie," We parted.

I turned into the immense lounge with its clusters of overstuffed furniture, which one must cross in order to reach the main hall. At this hour it's usually deserted except for Lady Fanquill, having her doze by the baronial hearth.

She is an elderly Strathburne relative who seems to be a permanent guest in the castle. Snowy-haired, she drapes her fragile aristocratic bones in chiffon scarves, lace, mohair, cashmere, and other gossamer materials which the slightest motion sets afloat. She could be mistaken for the castle ghost, drifting about on her appointed rounds — to the corner of the lounge after breakfast, out to the courtyard before lunch for a teetery stroll on the arm of the lad, up to her room for a siesta until teatime, and so on.

As I made my way silently over the carpet she opened her eyes and said, "I never could wear it myself."

I changed course and crossed the room to her. "What could you never wear, Lady Fanquill?"

"I had pink hair," she told me composedly, "and voilet quenched me." She was talking, I realized, about the color of my suit. "Sit down, my dear, but only for a moment, I am not up to prolonged tête-à-têtes in the morning. Utterly quenched me." Her speech is a murmur and her light blue eyes are vaguely unfocused and her lips curve in a faint satirical smile. It is disturbing to imagine her utterly quenched when she is so insubstantial to begin with. And rather profanely I wondered how the late Lord Fanquill managed to come to grips with her in their marriage bed. "You are Mrs. Barton MacLarkie, are you not? You have brought your sister-in-law and your nurse from America," she murmured on. "Does my nephew know you are here?"

I lowered myself to the cushions beside her but perched there on the alert. Following Lady Fanquill in however brief a tête-à-tête demands all one's powers of concentration. "Your nephew, Lady Fanquill?"

"The Earl, my dear, the Earl of Strathburne. You do know you are in his castle, do you not?"

"Of course, but I did not know he was your nephew." I drop my own voice when I am with her and articulate each word without contractions as she does. "No, I do not think he knows I am here." Why should he, I wondered? "I have not yet met him."

"True," said Lady Fanquill, "he does not mingle with the guests. I wonder if Jean neglected to tell him." Jean is the girl in charge of the reception desk in the main hall. Lady

Fanquill ruminated, her eyes encompassing me. I felt quite out of my depth. She is like an oracle, speaking in riddles. "Ah well," she said, "you seem a very decent sort to me. When you do meet him remember this: he is not unkind." She mused again. "Even though," she added, "he has had his share of unkindness." And with that she closed her eyes and dozed off again.

I studied her delicate, shuttered face for a moment. I tried to picture her with pink hair. No doubt there was some significance behind her esoteric questions and answers but I wasn't up to deciphering them. There was nothing to do but go on about my business.

I hoisted myself to my feet and resumed my way to the hall.

II. . . .

Jean saluted me from behind her mahogany counter. She's in her twenties, unmarried, with freckles and short-cropped red-gold hair, a crisp, efficient lassie who manages reservations, bills, correspondence, and telephone, as well as importunate or lustful grouse shooters, without ever seeming to lose her cool. "A braw day, I doubt!" Here they say I doubt when they mean *I don't doubt.*

"It makes up for the dour ones, doesn't it?" I answered. Sometimes I think Jean makes a

23

special effort for me, perhaps because of our nearness in age. She rises from her ledgers and comes forward to give me her full attention.

"I'm happy to hear you say so, Mrs. MacLarkie. Our reputation for dourness is well-founded, considering we get all the weather left over from the Atlantic and the Western Isles, to say nothing of the North Sea. My father believes it's responsible for the dauntless Scots character. We may have originated the saying, Make hay while the sun shines."

"That's just what I had in mind. I'm off for a great walk — down to the bridge and back!" It's a distance of about a hundred yards.

She's too nice to chime in with my self-ridicule. "Oh, very good! Enjoy yourself" Her telephone rang and I moved on.

Severn, Munro's helper, the youth known as the lad, came to attention as I approached his station, halfway down the hall, and he gave me his captivating smile. How old is he — fourteen, fifteen? Anyway, a very young teenager, younger in every way than an American boy of the same age. He carries bags and runs errands with remarkable earnestness — remarkable to me, used to the halfhearted, half-contemptuous performance of menial tasks in the States. Slight of build, Severn has brilliant hair like Jean's, and an exquisite complexion. But unlike the cool and collected lass, Severn has, so to speak, two sets of blushes — one on the top of his cheekbones and the other lower down, along the jawline, and one or the other set is always in evidence; on occasion, when he's flustered or earnest in the extreme, they both appear at the same time. And superimposed on these double blooms he has several attractively placed moles. A braw lad, and soon to be very much of a braw man.

He held back deferentially until I'd spoken first, and then burst out, "I was hoping ye'd be going out the day, mistress!" The day means today, and the Highlanders speak with a special cadence which must be a Gaelic hand-me-down. "Ye'll take pleasure in the sunshine!"

"I shall, Severn, with body and soul."

Perhaps the mention of *body* embarrassed him, for the top blushes glimmered in his cheekbones. At times, menial employment aside, he has quite a patrician look — something about the beautiful skin, the lengthening bones, and ease of stance. You can picture him in eighteenth-century Scottish dress like the bygone earls of Strathburne whose portraits hang in the lounge.

He said, "Ye'll be careful on the cobble-stones? Would ye like me to assist you?"

"No, thanks, I wouldn't. Because between

you and me, Severn, I want to try myself out. That's why Mrs. O'Halloran isn't with me. I am launching myself, this fine day, like a ship."

He gave way to a chuckle, and then, conscious that Munro, waiting at the big double doors, might think it overly familiar, stifled it. "Happy sailing," he said softly, as if we shared a delicious secret, and added with respect, "Mrs. MacLarkie."

I moved on. Munro threw open one of the immense doors. The sunlight poured in, and we chatted a moment about the peaceful beauty of the Highlands. "It's hard to believe," I said, "that it was ever necessary to build fortresses like this."

"Och, aye," he answered balefully. He is elderly, with white hair, but strong and wiry. I can't transpose his accent to paper, indeed I can scarcely understand more than one word in ten. Jean and Severn speak with the national burr but Munro overlays it with heavy Gaelic incrustations. "When the Highlanders weren't fighting the English," he told me — I figured out — "they were fighting themselves. Aye, blood has been shed here!" The sunlight didn't feel as warm, suddenly.

He lent me a steadying hand down the steps and off I went across the courtyard, a cobbled enclosure large enough to hold a small army of horsemen, but prettied up now with a patch of lawn and a formal arrangement of geraniums and rose trees.

Structurally the castle must be little altered from its earliest days. Och, aye, it wouldn't be easy to alter, with walls four feet thick. It stands on a point of land that was once an island, and when you first emerge from the mountain pass at the other end of the loch it looks spellbound, its tawny ramparts brooding over the still dark water, and you might think you'd come upon an enchanted glen unmarked on any map. After the clans were subdued by the English, or subdued each other, the castle was made accessible to the mainland by a bridge and a short causeway, themselves now a couple of hundred years old.

I went through the arched portal and headed down the ramp where once a drawbridge must have hung over a moat. On my right the drive hugged the castle walls and curved around to the garage, out of sight behind a drum tower. On my left lay the margin of land under the south walls which has been terraced and made into a garden with gravel walks and wooden seats. Dahlias and mums and roses as large as soup plates riot in the sun. (None of the guidebooks prepared me for the flowers of Scotland.) And there on a wooden bench sat

Lilah, her back to me.

I opened my mouth to halloo, then held back the sound. She was not needlepointing, for once, but sitting straight-backed, staring before her. What was she looking at? She's not a bird-watcher, and anyway I could see nothing stirring in the garden before her. She must have been pondering something. But what thoughts made gentle Lilah so tense, sitting bolt upright without moving a muscle? It was almost alarming.

Was she making plans to leave Scotland after all? Worrying about the future? But she knows I will never let her want for anything, as Bart never did. Andrew's share of the family fortune went into some poor investments – in fact, Bart was the only one of the three brothers who inherited their grandfather's canny business head. So after Andrew's death Bart set up a trust for Lilah, to supplement her small income. She protested, with tears in her eyes, and perhaps in a way it was mortifying to her, but Bart put a great arm around her, reminding her with a grin that he never took no for an answer. His generosity was genuine, and he harbored no sense of anyone's indebtedness to him.

I moved on down the ramp, puzzled by Lilah, feeling I mustn't intrude on her. I looked back before she was lost to sight behind the garden wall. Her spine had relaxed, her head was bent once more over her canvas. Had she come to a decision? I gave myself a little shake as though to ward off gooseflesh. If someone, I thought, were to watch me when I didn't know I was being watched, they'd no doubt find my behavior mystifying. I turned away and continued along the causeway

Now the panorama of blue-green hills opened around me, the air so limpid that the far peaks and the fir trees on their flanks were finely detailed as if seen through powerful binoculars. I rested my forearms on the wide stone balustrade of the hump-backed bridge and gazed up the length of the loch, gratefully inhaling the mingled sun-warmed fragrances of earth and water. The man-of-all-work in kilts was rowing toward a distant shore. There was an almost total absence of sound, and the upland bowl seemed absorbed in its own enchantment.

It occurred to me suddenly that a portion of this scenery might belong to me. Or was it what was left of the original Strathburne estate? I hadn't given thought yet to anything as mundane as ownership; I planned eventually to take my legal documents to Kirkangus, the nearest town, and seek out a law firm to locate the acres for me.

If Lord Greggan, ninth Earl of Strathburne,

were disposed to mingle with his guests, I might have sought the information from him, but kind though he may be he keeps to himself in a separate wing of the castle, and who can blame him. It can't be agreeable to have to turn one's ancestral home over to indifferent yet exacting strangers.

Noise intruded after all, a growing guttural snarl, and a red sports car came bucketing down the loch road. It turned into the causeway and approached the bridge, where brakes were suddenly applied, bringing it to a gravel-scraping halt alongside me.

Jock, the castle's lively young major domo, raised his checked sports cap straight up a couple of inches and resettled it on his thick auburn curls. He wore a smartly fitted checked jacket and as he smiled he was very much the toff, elegant and sexy, well-mannered and self-contained, but quite willing, plainly, to go as far with a woman as he was encouraged to do.

As major domo, one might say factotum, within the castle, he is all punctilio, skillfully pouring drinks in the bar while making easy small talk, then donning a dark blazer over his red bartender's vest to preside over the dining room, where he swoops about as though on ice skates, deftly avoiding the backsides of bending waitresses. Always keeping his own counsel, he

30

supplies travel information and local lore, intro-
duces strangers to each other and creates an
atmosphere of bonhomie, and late in the evening,
I deduce from the faint commotion reaching my
room before the bar shuts down, sings.

But he has a way with the women, obviously.
He keeps the waitresses stifling giggles. When
he's finished pouring our wine Dottie O. gives
me a kind of squinting, nostril-flaring leer that
convulses me. Even Lady Fanquill becomes
conquettish as he lends her his arm to escort
her to and from her table.

Only Jean at the desk seems unmoved by
him, like a sister, or a girl who's been through a
romance with him and got over it. But I
sometimes wonder if her casual, rather caustic
manner is a trifle studied and if she's as indifferent to him as she's determined to appear.

"A perfect day to be out of doors," he told me,
idly shifting gears with his foot on the clutch
while the engine burbled. "I'm glad to see you
taking advantage —"

A breeze had come up, ruffling the lake, and
I tossed back the hair that brushed across my
face. His voice died and for a second he lost his
savoir faire and stared.

I know this stare. Bart himself gave way to it,
when he chanced to visit me, editor of his
newsletter, in my cubbyhole on the nineteenth

floor of the MacLarkie Building: I looked up, preoccupied, and whatever he was going to say died on his lips. "Wow!" Dottie exclaimed, the first time I put on a little makeup, and then, "Far be it from me to mention men at this point in your life, but you better believe they aren't gonna leave you alone, not with your looks."

But "looks" contain their own built-in hazards, I learned long ago as a teenager; they bring about their own quarantine. Perhaps what's needed is a healthy ego to match; but I had spent too many years as the belated child of awesomely intellectual parents for an ego of my own. Overnight, almost, "looks" made my own darling absent-minded-professor father shy with me, and my brilliant mother distant. Girl friends left me out of things, boys no longer teased and rough-and-tumbled. I felt stranded on an uninhabited island.

And it was then, I expect, that I developed the hopeful expression, and acquired a kind of self-eclipsing blur, and to this day only an inadvertent toss of the head or a preoccupied lift of the face from a desk or a bit of makeup can cause that sudden astonished arrest of a man's eyes.

"But it's a responsibility!" Colin MacLarkie protested. He was holding forth to Bart and me not about my looks but what he called outright my beauty. Traditionally Colin was the brazen one of the brothers. "Any woman with raven hair, alabaster skin, and longlashed, smoke-colored eyes" — he dwelt on the words unabashedly, knowing he was abashing me — "should thank God and make the most of it!" Colin, inveterate bachelor, had a period of mock-infatuation with me while Bart still lived; he acted it up for a while and it was a family joke.

"Cut it out, Colin," said Bart, laughing. "You'll drive Susan away." He enfolded my hand in his enormous one. "She makes enough of herself to suit me." I leaned my head against his shoulder. Yes, I had the kind of ego that took to being enfolded, to suiting, and Bart was never happier than when enfolding.

Jock, in his grumbling sports car, stared only for a second and then pulled his face together and made a quick half-apologetic grin. He frowned at the dashboard, still smiling. He turned to me again, sitting so low in the little car that he had to look up at me. "Yes, well, any time I can be of service to you, Mrs. MacLarkie, I'd be only too happy to oblige."

Was that a trifle obvious? But on such a morning, in such sunlight, one couldn't hunt for double meanings. He was more of the tailwagging sort than the taloned. I was in fact finding it hard not to smile back at him with the come-on he hoped for, giving him the inch he needed to translate into a mile. "That's kind of you, Mr. – uh – Jock."

"Thornhill. Gordon Thornhill. I'm a distant cousin of the laird's. It's a family affair, you see, the castle hotel, though I live in Kirkangus. I call myself Jock because it's easy for our guests to remember and so all-purpose Scottish." He squinted into the sun. "Or, as you Americans say, Scotch."

"If you want an all-purpose Scottish image, shouldn't you wear kilts?"

"A kilt," Jock said. "You are wearing a skirt today, not skirts. In fact, those of us with Nationalist leanings call it *the* kilt. Well, I do wear the kilt on dress occasions, but for the run-of-the-mill working day it would be rather like a Texan wearing a Stetson and highheeled boots to the office."

"Probably lots of Texans do."

"Aye, and Scottish diehards, particularly among the nobility, cling to the kilt for daily wear, and I'll mention no names." He settled the gear shift for real. "And speaking of work, I'd best get on to it, though given the choice I'd far rather spend the morning nattering with a gorgeous girl. See you at lunch, shall I?"

"As you Scots say, I doubt."

"Correct," he nodded approvingly, and grasping the peak of his checked cap he raised it straight up again. "Good-bye, Mrs. MacLarkie, for now, and if I may make up an old Scottish farewell, may the sun always shine in your hair," With an explosive roar the little car leaped forward, gravel flew, and he sped off up the last half of the causeway. He took the branch of the drive that led around to the garage.

I turned about. The handyman in the skiff had vanished from sight, and I was alone in the Glen's great stillness.

A familiar terrible desolation threatened to fall over me like the darkness of night. The futile lashing penance began: Oh God, Bart, if only we'd stayed home, if only we hadn't been rounding the curve when the brakes gave, if only I'd reminded you to fasten your seat belt — ! For an instant hills, loch, sky, crumpled before my eyes, and I saw once again the canyon yawning beneath us as we went over, heard the final ghastly sounds, the final cries . . .

But this sickening descent of the spirit I've learned to control.

Scowling, grinding my teeth, coughing away sobs, I fought off the blinding dissolution, leaned on the parapet, and glared at the ruffled sparkling water.

Is this what an innocent flirtation, even a

would-be flirtation, leads to?

Then there was a soft, almost stealthy touch on my arm, and with a gasp I whirled about.

III. . . . .

"It's only me, dear." Lilah peered anxiously into my face. She knows what the clenched jaw and tautly drawn throat mean, even though she hasn't seen me go through a spell like this in quite a while. "I've been in the rose garden. I was just going in when I spied you here."

The blood rushed downward, seemingly, from my forehead, flooding my face, and a great breath escaped me, and I laughed to cover the pressing storm of tears. "Oh, Lilah," I dithered hoarsely, "isn't it beautiful? Isn't it the most beautiful day?"

"Yes, darling. Yes. It certainly is. I'm glad to see you out in it. Yes, it's beautiful." Thus, dithering back, she tries to comfort. One word of pity would undo me. "Shall we walk a little farther?" Wordlessly I pressed her hand between mine. "Or, no, look," she went on, "there are two dear little boats at the end of the bridge, they must be for hotel guests. Shall we row out on the loch? I'm sure I can remember how to row, and the boats are flat-bottomed, they must be perfectly safe. Shall we try it?"

Then I should have had the wits to say no to

her, for once. But she looked so eagerly into my face, like a child, and I seized on the distraction. Deep down I may still have been concerned about her, after seeing her in the rose garden. I have only myself to blame. "All right, Lilah, let's try it."

We giggled a lot, I remember, over our clumsiness in getting underway – my awkward crawl to the stern, while Lilah tried to place the oars in the oarlocks and cast off, but at last we managed to pull away from the little stone wharf.

For a few minutes I was delighted. Despite Lilah's weak rowing strokes we made progress, heading into the breeze, and presently we were looking back on the castle as it stood up against the blue sky, its flag whipping and the sun making sharp shadows in its angled towers and overhanging battlements. Lilah and I smiled, facing each other.

I tried the water with my hand and withdrew it quickly as if I'd plunged it into a pitcher of ice water. Cold as a tomb, Munro had said.

"Are you chilly, dear?" Lilah asked.

I was hugging myself. "Not really, Lilah. Are you sure this isn't too much for you?"

"Oh no," she exclaimed, her face alight. "I love it, don't you?"

"Yes, it's delightful, but do turn back when

you begin to tire."

The wind was sharper and the water rougher than had appeared from the bridge. The boat slapped the wavelets as we bounced along, sending back little showers. The loch seemed larger. I could look down the length of it, perhaps a mile.

Lilah glanced over her shoulder now and then but it didn't matter, really, where she was going, because there was almost unlimited space around us. The boat was headed obliquely toward the uninhabited shore on the far side, a shore of ragged inlets, dark ledges, and fir trees that dropped steeply down from the hills. At the slow rate we were going we would never reach it before Lilah tired.

Yet I felt the first stirrings of fear. I told myself there was nothing to be afraid of but I had a premonition of calamity. It may have stemmed from Munro and his direful, "Och, aye, bottomless," and the bell note of omen in his voice. "Lilah," I said at last, "I *am* getting cold. Let's turn back."

"Of course, dear."

We rolled precariously as we came about and I gripped the edges of my seat, almost level with the gunwales. I was terrified of losing my balance. We were moving very fast now, down wind.

"You'll have to keep bearing on your right oar," I cautioned Lilah, "so that we don't get blown onto the rocks!"

She was already somewhat flustered, for the wind had definitely picked up. "Yes, I'm trying, dear!"

I saw, dead ahead of us, half-buried in the brisk waves, what looked like a buoy with a faded topping of red paint. I made a last effort to keep my voice calm. "Lilah, turn, turn away, I think I see a marker."

My warning may have come too late in any case. Her face paled, and she grasped both oars and gave a mighty, panic-stricken heave, and we rammed the hidden rocks with a bone-jarring crash. The boat lifted and then righted itself, but the impact had wrenched my hands free of the seat and I went over into the water.

From that moment I can recall only a kaleidoscopic confusion – the icy breathtaking shock of the water engulfing me, the sun making dazzling patterns over my head as I struggled, choking, to regain the surface, the boat moving fast away from me. I must have cleared the surface at least once for I remember a glimpse of Lilah's ashen face, receding as the distance widened between us, and her open mouth working as if she were screaming. I thought if I could find a footing on the rocks we'd run into

I might save myself, but my legs were helpless and my wool suit acted as a weight.

My lungs could no longer take in air and I fought with my entire body to get a breath. A voice, my own voice, was crying, yet not making a sound. Bart, I said, as I struggled in silence, I'm dying too, now, I'm drowning . . .

The edges of the world, sunlight and water, began to close darkly over me.

There were final bits and pieces of consciousness. Or do I only think I was conscious and imagine what followed — the powerful arms grasping me, being heaved head first into a strange boat, being roughly tumbling over on the floorboards?

Last of all, in the winking, shrinking kaleidoscope, I looked up into fierce blue eyes and a mouth close to mine, and then the darkness closed in entirely.

CHAPTER 3

I. . . .

I came to in my bed, in my castle bedroom. A nice, serious-looking young man, not very tall, held my wrist with a professional thumb-and-forefinger grasp, while Dottie O. frowned over his shoulder. It was the warmth that brought me wallowing up to consciousness, the delicious benevolent warmth invading me slowly on all sides, and I realized I was banked with hot water bottles, even to the soles of my feet.

"*Well*," I commenced, intending to say I know not what, but the word ended in a gurgle and at once I began to retch up loch water. Dottie held a handy basin for me and when the spasm was over I sank back and felt relieved. The pleasant man, who looked old before his time, bore down upon me with a stethoscope.

"She'll do," he said at last, straightening, and I knew from his heavy double *l*s and abbreviated *dew* that I was alive in Scotland. He pocketed his stethoscope and turned to consult with Dottie O.

Before I closed my eyes again I saw in a corner of the room the hunched, plump figure of Lilah. Her face was buried in her hands.

I'm alive after all, Bart, I said, again in silence. Good-bye again.

I wasn't sorry; the will to survive insisted on its triumph. The warmth of life takes precedence over the cold of death. But I was weary of recurring narrow squeaks; it would almost be less of an ordeal to lose the battle.

"Unless she shows signs of . . ." It was all familiar, the voices whispering in the background. ". . . as well off here with you as . . . hospital clinic . . . but let me know if . . ."

The woolly warmth enfolded me and I drowsed.

My lamp was lighted when I awoke. Dottie was sitting beside my bed. "What time is it?"

Dottie looked at her watch. "Half past six."

"Half past six when? What day?"

"Jesus God, kiddo, the same day as you went to sleep. How do you feel?"

I propped myself on my elbows. Lilah was no longer in the room. "I feel hungry. And I'm sweltering, can I take some of these blankets

42

off? And, oh Lord," I flopped back again, "I'd better hear what happened."

Dottie got up and started peeling off blankets. "What happened was you took a row on the lake like a damn fool and got dumped overboard."

"I know that. We ran into some rocks, we didn't see the marker in time. But then what?"

"The man who goes out fishing every day hauled you out. He was in some cove nearby, at least near enough so you didn't quite drown. If it hadn't been for him giving you first aid, you wouldn't be alive. Then Jean called this Dr. Craigie in Kirkangus; good man. Looks like no real damage was done, but it was a close shave. What ever possessed you, Sue-baby, doing a crazy thing like that, going out on an icy-cold lake when you still can't swim?"

"Ah, Dottie, don't scold!"

"Was it Lilah's idea?" Dottie was rummaging in my bed for hot water bottles.

"She only wanted to cheer me up, take my mind off . . . I was having one of my, you know, one of my bad spells. Poor Lilah, is she crushed?"

"Poor Lilah," said Dottie flatly. "Yeah, she's crushed." And Dottie popped a thermometer in my mouth.

A little later Jean came in. Bright as a marigold, she crossed the room, touched my hand, and said, "I'm so glad you're all right!"

I thanked her for sending for Dr. Craigie and expressed regret at having caused a fuss. "You must have rounded up every hot water bottle in the place."

"Aye, and some of the vintage stone ones I'd forgotten we had." Jean turned deferentially to Dottie. "What would Mrs. MacLarkie like for supper?"

I said I was well enough to get dressed and go down to dinner, but Dottie gave an incontestable "Ha!" and ordered for me.

As Jean reached the door I said, "I'll thank the man who rescued me — you know, the blond fisherman — as soon as I'm able."

Jean turned with a twinkle. "That is my father. I'm glad he was near at hand." And she left.

My supper of beef broth and hot tea and toast restored me to normal, and I was settling back for another snooze when Lilah knocked. Dottie admitted her without a word, then went into her adjoining room, leaving the door open. Lilah sat down by my bed, her face already crumpling. "Oh, Susan!"

I decided it would ease her mind to cry it out, so I patted her hands and let her sob. Dottie in the next room cleared her throat to inform me I had only to signal and she would come charging in and break it up.

"Oh, Sue, I should never . . . but how could I know it would turn so rough . . . and then the rocks . . . and the wind carried me away from you . . . it was like one of those nightmares where you feel absolutely helpless . . . Oh, I'll never forgive myself!"

"Well, you must, darling. It's over and done with. Dr. Craigie is coming back tomorrow but I know he'll find me none the worse for wear. You're not to blame, Lilah, it was just bad luck."

She left at last, blowing her nose and only partially consoled.

Dottie returned at once, her mouth clamped shut on what might have been withering words, and went about getting me settled for the night.

I anticipated a deep and peaceful sleep. I felt thankful, warm, safe, and well. But my dreams, it turned out, were troubled.

Defenseless and alone, I fled from an invisible menace that shadowed every scene. I recognized it; it had been there before and it would be there again. And yet I couldn't see its face. I'm not dreaming, I kept telling myself, I really am dying this time!

And at the last minute I looked hopelessly into a pair of fierce blue eyes.

Dr. Craigie went painstakingly over my chest and back, my throat and eyes and ears and arms and legs, and finally sat back, saying, "Ye wouldn't say ye feel better for it, would ye?"

I laughed. "I would, almost."

I was free to leave my room, and I dressed for lunch.

As I made my way to the dining room with Dottie and Lilah I was welcomed like an astronaut after a succesful reentry. Jean, Severn, and Munro congratulated me. Even Lady Fanquill floated up to quaver, "My dear, can it be you?"

She seemed really to want to know, and for a disoriented moment so did I. The conviction of death in my dreams still haunted me. "Yes," I assured her gently, "I believe it is."

"Ah," she sighed. "I *am* pleased. One cannot help liking you." And she floated away again.

I gave my head a little shake to rid it of cobwebs (had she for some reason tried not to like me?) and caught up with Dottie and Lilah.

The English couple who do not shoot but do a great deal of walking and eating stopped at our table. "Happy to see you about!" barked Mrs. Barsington-Banks, a commanding woman who always looks drawn up to receive a medal. "Mustn't give in! Mustn't go soft! Cold baths never hurt anyone!"

Major Barsington-Banks took time to press my shoulder and utter his single word, which seemed to cover every occasion: *"Rum!"* And he scurried off to seat his lady.

"Jesus God," muttered Dottie, "I betcha she picks him up and tosses him into a cold bath every morning."

We were as usual in the small dining room, furnished with red leather chairs and red tablecloths. Windows have been cut – with the aid of dynamite I should think – into the ancient stone to open a view of the loch and the hills. The larger dining room next door is the original refectory, a vaulted hall capable of seating a couple of hundred, its walls hung with old banners and imaginative implements of slaughter and self-preservation from the days of Scottish mayhem. Jean told me they use the hall only for bus tours in summer and the odd convention, when they "lay on the pipers in a gr-r-and Scots do."

Jock attended us solicitously. Would we care for more soup? Would we take our coffee now? (He indulges our American habit of taking coffee with lunch rather than afterward in the lounge.) Was the air from the open window too cool for me?

Dottie, watching him dart away, narrowed

her eyes and said, "I think he's got a crush on you, Susan."

"Oh, hush, Dottie," said Lilah with a tiny giggle. I was glad to see her recovering from her misery.

"Why?" Dottie shrugged. "Any reason why he shouldn't?"

"No, but, well, after all . . ."

"You mean it's too soon for Susan to think about sex?" Dottie reminds me of the character in a Somerville and Ross novel who "habitually said what other people hardly dared to think." She blundered on, "Baloney." Her slang has the dated naiveté of an earlier era. "I'm not saying Susan should hop into bed with a good-looking maitre d', but you can't expect her to carry a torch forever, can you?"

"*Really*, Dottie," Lilah closed her eyes as I'd seen her do when Colin MacLarkie said something outrageous. But she giggled again. "Don't let her lead you astray, Susan."

I patted her arm. "Don't worry. Dottie's an incurable romantic, that's all."

"Sure hope so," grumped Dottie. "Don't wanta be cured." She had sat up most of the night with me; no doubt she was having one of her headaches.

When Jock recommended the sweet for dessert, a confection of meringue and almonds, telling us, "Cook invented it specially for a slender, sloe-eyed Persian princess," I had to laugh, as he must have intended me to. The castle cook is fine with native dishes like salmon and mutton and baps and rumbledethump, but not very successful with inventions or confections, and if there'd ever been a Persian princess in this unlikely place, I'd eat my hat.

"Boy, if he slender, sloe-eyed Persian princessed *me*," sighed Dottie, as Jock went off to see to our orders, "I might have a hard time remembering pear-shaped, flat-footed Sam, back home."

III. . . .

After lunch Dottie made me promise to rest and went to her room for a nap.

Lilah turned to me. "I thought if you didn't mind I'd take the car, Susan, and practice driving on the left side of the road."

"By all means, Lilah, try it out. I've been meaning to go to Kirkangus soon." I'd hired a professional driver to bring us up from Glasgow, and sent him back by bus. He was a careful driver but I was a sorry wreck by the time we got here. Ever since the accident with Bart, riding in a car has been traumatic for me, and I'd postponed even a short trip to the

49

nearby town. "I'll see you at teatime," I told her.

It was nearly four o'clock when I got up from my rest. I put on a warm sweater and went down to the reception desk to ask Jean where I might find her father. Today I thought I saw a blue-eyed, golden-haired resemblance, although I'd had only the most fragmentary glimpse of her father.

She seemed pleased that I wanted to seek him out and thank him personally for his first aid. "I'm not sure where you'll find him, he moves about so, and when you can't find him it may mean he doesn't wish to be found." She held her breath for an instant like a person who is about to give a word of caution but thinks better of it. "You might try the old stable yard first, just past the garage, and you can shorten the distance by going through the castle. No, no, you mustn't go alone! The lad will show you. Severn!"

Severn came at once to my side, his stature miraculously increasing from idle five-foot-seven to enthusiastic five-foot-eight or nine. We proceeded from the hall into a service corridor, noisy with the clatter of the adjacent kitchen, and on through another door. A flight of dimly lighted stone steps lead downward into a stone passage. Severn grasped my arm protectively, and we descended into the ancient substructure of the castle.

"You know the place like the back of your hand, I suppose, Severn?"

"Not altogether, mistress. Only the laird knows all the chambers here below. I used to explore them when I was a wee lad but I got thrashed for it." His lower, or jawline, blushes came and went. "It's dangerous to explore alone."

We had leveled off and were heading along still another passage, this one curving, narrow, and damp. The only light now was the daylight filtering through slits high in the wall. I figured we were rounding a tower on the one-time moat; there was a shelf under the narrow slits for archers to stand on. "Why dangerous, Severn?"

"Why, because the chambers below are dark and you could get lost in the maze, and there are open drops and even a great round hole in the floor over the stream that empties into the loch, for dumping bodies into. It's forbidden for anyone to venture beyond the wine cellar."

There was still a sinister emanation from the damp stonework, even centuries after its use in battle; a permanent grim taint of carnage. Blood, as Munro had pointed out, had been shed here.

We were climbing upward again, into further

51

passages, Severn very much the young knight guiding a lady, taking long slow strides. "Would you like to rest a moment, mistress?"

"No, let's go on." It wasn't a place I wanted to tarry in.

We stopped at last before a heavy oaken door, which Severn pushed open. The stable yard lay before us, a long cobbled quadrangle of box stalls, separated from the shed where guests stored their cars by a Gothic arch, its keystone carved with the Strathburne coat of arms.

At the far end of the quadrangle the man-of-all-work was hosing down a car.

"There he is," said Severn, "with the Lagonda. Ye'll want me to wait and show you the way back, won't you?"

"No, thank you, Severn, I'll walk around outside by the way of the drive." I had no desire to return to the cellars of Strathburne. "Every foot of mileage helps."

"Aye, mistress." He heaved an unconscious sigh. "Well, then, I must leave you." He stepped back, hesitating, as if about to make a low bow; but he must have decided that was going too far, and gave me instead his winning smile, accompanied by his upper blushers, and turned and retreated at a run the way he'd come.

The kilted man had his back to me and hadn't heard us over the spatter of the hose. For a moment I didn't move. I liked this place, the cool secluded courtyard with the sun slanting on the leaded windows of the medieval living quarters above the stalls, the pots of geraniums. I liked very much being befriended by a teenager. I liked being called mistress.

And thus, full of confidence, I set out for the man at work on the car.

It was a grand old vehicle, the Lagonda, silver-gray, with the mellow, lovingly crafted texture of fine European cars. The man turned off the hose by the nozzle, dropped it, and took up a chamois, his motions careful and unhurried, and then he spied me and wheeled about to face me, and I looked once more into the piercing blue eyes.

He is younger, somewhere in his forties, than he appears from a distance, and he is not bearded but in need of a shave and a haircut. Yellow whiskers curl all over him, face, ears, and neck; even his sturdy knees between stockings and kilt are covered with golden down. His threadbare tartan was one of subdued browns and grays with a stripe of moss green, the Strathburne tartan, presumably, the same tartan the waitresses wear in the dining room, and above it he had on a dark flannel shirt with the sleeves rolled up over muscular, fleecy arms.

It was a strange silence that held us for a

moment, a silence that stopped me because there was no welcome in the blue eyes and I didn't understand the absence of cordiality. I could only surmise he resented having had to plunge into frigid water to rescue a foolhardy American tourist, and my confident mood dwindled to a state of apology.

I cleared my throat at last. The world over, I told myself, dredging up self-esteem, there were quirky, waspish people, even in Scotland. I forced an ingratiating smile. "I came to thank you. I owe you my life and I'm very grateful."

He gave a short nod. "Aye, then, no more need be said." His eyes never wavered and now that I'd spoken and he'd answered the eyes dismissed me. He waited for me to depart.

If only I'd left it at that! But like a child who must win a token of favor, I blundered on. "If there is any way I can recompense you –"

The color of his eyes seemed to deepen. "What d'you mean: you'd pay me?"

"Of course." I was a little short of breath, my state of apology heading further downward toward chagrin. It was the kind of situation Bart handled with such ease, slipping dollars into empty hands without anyone's suffering embarrassment. I felt a stir of baffled resentment on my own part because I couldn't seem to do the gracious thing with this surly rustic, and I wondered how he'd reared as outgoing a girl as Jean. No doubt he was useful about the castle, supplying fish and game, tending the rose garden, washing the laird's car (as I assumed it to be), but it was fortunate that his contact with the hotel guests was minimal.

I faltered, "I don't quite know what you would consider sufficient —"

He gave a muted derisive bark. "Well, I thank you, madam, but I find it impossible to put a monetary value on human life." How much more homey mistress was than madam! And even in my bewilderment I was aware he sounded much more literate now than rustic. "How would you appraise yourself?" he demanded. "Ten thousand pounds? A million dollars? No, it can't be done. Even you could not afford it." He turned his back then, since he couldn't get rid of me any other way, and set to work polishing the chromium trim with his chamois.

"Nevertheless," I persisted, determined not to allow the mission to end on such an unpleasant note, or perhaps merely to have the last word, lowering my chin into my collar and addressing him in a rather schoolteachery tone while my throat betrayed me hoarsely, "nevertheless it was a selfless and very quick-witted thing you did, and I'm beholden to you —"

"Aye, aye," he said, cutting me short and working away. "I accept your thanks though I do not require them. Good day."

I couldn't help myself. My face, I knew, was scarlet, and I felt the starry, headachy prickle behind the eyes that precedes tears.

"I don't know why you are so hostile," I told him, "but you are making me feel hostile, too. I mean, I can understand your despising a silly woman you've had to pull out of the loch, but I don't see that you have a right to be insulting when she comes to thank you. Are you rude to everyone or only to women?"

After that, admittedly, I deserved what I got. He put down his chamois and wheeled about again, eyes blazing, planting his fists on the wide belt clasping his hips. "Mrs. MacLarkie!" He uttered the name as if it were an imprecation. "I pulled you out of the loch not knowing who you were. I didn't find out until after I'd brought you ashore. I gave you the kiss of life, did you know that? And I'd have done the same for anyone, man or woman. It didn't occur to me to put a price on the act. And when I learned who you were it didn't make me wish I'd left you to drown."

I gasped. "But why ever should it? You don't know me at all! What have you got against me?"

Perhaps this cry of utter bafflement penetrated his crust more than a well-phrased tongue-lashing. It jarred him. And I saw now that his eyes looked at me through a suffering of his own, having nothing to do with me, and at that look of pain and pride my anger evaporated and I was filled with remorse. I had a sudden and irrational and almost irresistible desire to step forward and put my arms around this strapping, muscular man, a primitive female urge, and with my softer body warm and soothe him, release him from his private anguish.

"Perhaps there are two kinds of charity," he said, recalling me to reality. His voice had dropped to a more reasonable level, although weary and harsh. "The charity of the purse and the charity of the heart. Your late husband requested we be notified that the MacLarkie land here – the poacher's paradise, we call it – is to be returned to Strathburne on your death. I'd say the score is even, wouldn't you? Take your time, madam, take a long look at your neglected land, and fly back to America, and God keep you in good health."

We were done with each other at last. "Yes," I said, nodding, tears standing in my eyes. "And meanwhile I will certainly try to stay out of your way and cause you no more aggravation. Good-bye."

He must have seen me then for the first time, his eyes coming into focus with quick questioning pupils. Involuntarily he reached out to detain me.

But I had moved away, turning toward the Gothic gate. Then certain clues and bits of information fell into place, as they should have before this, and I looked back and asked, already guessing the answer, "What is your name, by the way?"

"Greggan," he said, with a kind of bitter resignation, "of Strathburne." And he faced about once more to minister to his antiquated motorcar.

CHAPTER 4

I. . . . .

Lilah was waiting for me by the hearth in the lounge, a tea tray set before her. The boisterous grouse hunters hadn't yet returned and you could hear a clock tick in the enormous room. Lady Fanquill had evidently finished her tea and wandered off, for her corner on the opposite side of the hearth was deserted, but the Barsington-Bankses occupied one of the large bays overlooking the courtyard, where they sipped in silence. A consecrated hour, teatime, not sociable like the cocktail hour; we keep our voices low.

Lilah peered up at me. "Are you all right? You haven't walked too far?"

I must have looked somewhat shaken. "I need my tea, that's all." I dropped down beside her and gestured for her to pour. "Funny, isn't it, how we Americans get to depend on our tea here."

"Dottie's skipping hers. When I told her I'd

been practicing with the car, right away she had to go and practice herself." She made a burlesque face. "At least for once you and I are going to have a few moments to ourselves."

I try to ignore her dry remarks about Dottie. I was still trembling from my encounter with the laird.

But Lilah was suddenly grave. "Susan, you don't think Dottie's slightly over-possessive, do you?"

I looked at her, my cup halfway to my lips. "Of me, you mean?"

"I mean, she seems almost jealous where you're concerned. She tries to be so completely in charge."

"Lilah, she *is* in charge, that's what I pay her for." We were whispering. "I wouldn't have tried half as hard if she hadn't stood over me and goaded me. You're not implying she has lesbian tendencies?"

Lilah gulped and smothered a laugh. "Of course not. In fact she tends too much in the opposite direction. But, Susan, every now and then you read about a wealthy person who's been an invalid a long time and become very dependent on his nurse, who gradually takes over —"

"Oh, Lilah." I closed my eyes.

"I know, maybe I'm being absurd, but I have

to get this off my chest. I'm not saying Dottie is actually out to get control over you, but don't let her take too much into her own hands, that's all. It could happen without your realizing it. Don't let her become a fixture in your life."

"Lilah, that's the most ridiculous thing I've ever heard."

"Yes. I suppose I've put my foot in it; it wouldn't be the first time. But I had to warn you. I had to!"

I let it drop. I reached for a scone, and after a few seconds I asked her, "How did it go, driving on the left?"

"Why, there's nothing to it!" She brightened. "The only dangerous thing about it is the occasional sheep in the road."

"Good. We'll go to Kirkangus tomorrow. It's time we got away from the castle for a bit."

She looked at me sideways. "Which one of us will drive?"

I had to smile. "You shall drive going in, and Dottie will drive home."

Lilah turned to me, the little lines of rueful humor showing around her lips. "You have to treat me just like a child sometimes, don't you?"

She took me completely by surprise. I didn't know she permitted herself such insight or candor. Her sweet wistful smile *was* childish, and somehow incorrigible, as if she knew she disarmed me, and in my already unnerved state a prickle of gooseflesh rippled up my arms, the same sensation of alarm I'd had when I saw her brooding in the rose garden and began to realize a great part of Lilah is a mystery to me.

My affection and loyalty are too firmly established to allow this alien mistrust houseroom for more than an instant, but I answered wryly, "Yes, sometimes I do." I didn't feel up to denying the truth. "And I don't mind, if you don't." I took her hand and pressed it briefly to my cheek.

She dissolved into a little ripple of laughter, and then quieted an said, "Oh, Susan," and looked as if she might go off into self-recriminations about the boating accident again, so I hastily asked her if the car was easy to handle. She said it held the road well once you adjusted to the small wheelbase, but it had a stiff handbrake and a silly beep of a horn. We finished our tea, talking about her drive, and then she gathered herself to rise.

"I'll go up and have my lie-down before dinner. You should, too, shouldn't you, dear? It's awfully soon for you to be up and around after — after yesterday. Oh, wait a minute, I picked up the mail at the desk." She fished in her big tan traveling purse. "There's some business mail for you. I looked through it in case there was anything for me. Those lawyers never stop pestering you with papers to sign, do they? Oh, and you have a letter from Colin."

She gave me the bundle of mail and waited, watching my face. Perhaps she hoped I'd open Colin's letter immediately.

I said, "Thanks, darling," and pocketed the letters. I don't always satisfy her curiosity. But I was mildly curious myself. What was Colin writing me about? I'd seen little of him since Bart's death. I was surprised he knew of our whereabouts, although it would have been easy enough to trace me.

I got to my feet with Lilah. I wanted very much now to be alone, but I was afraid if I remained behind in the lounge the Barsington-Bankses might claim me. We went upstairs.

Once in my room I forgot about the letters, including the one from Colin. Probably I wanted to. Reminders from home, even impersonal communications from the lawyers handling Bart's estate, never fail to depress me. For the first time the present overshadowed the past.

I lay on my bed and tried to figure out Lord Greggan, Earl of Strathburne. Was he simply a type of dour Scots woman-hater? But his animosity was directed fairly unmistakably at me.

Was it the loss of land to Grandfather MacLarkie that made my name so offensive? But that transaction had taken place long ago, long before the present laird was born. Grandfather MacLarkie must have paid the old laird's asking price, and if blame were to be levied, then the old laird ought to share in it, too, at least a little. Does the loss of land mean eternal disgrace to a noble Scots family?

Lord Greggan had made the very point that troubled Bart: the land's neglect. Perhaps that was what rankled so, the unforgivable insult of high-handed indifference added to the injury of appropriation.

I wondered if the irony of my rescue had struck Lord Greggan: if he had not given me the kiss of life, the MacLarkie land would now be his.

And what of my own feelings — that astonishing urge to take a step forward and embrace him? Perhaps this was a woman's conventional reaction to a woman-hater, an unthinking response to a challenge. There had been a maternal element in it, even one of pity.

Baloney, Dottie would have said. I was aroused, that's what. I was attracted to him, to the golden-haired masculinity of him. I wanted those powerful arms around me, that powerful body against mine.

I hardly knew myself. Small wonder I was still shaken. I was conditioned by my feelings for Bart, which as far as sex was concerned were as uncomplicated as the rest, my own satisfaction being less important to me than the pleasure of satisfying Bart.

Well, maybe this sudden arousal by Greggan of Strathburne was merely another sign of returning health, of glands and organs coming to life again in their own undisciplined fashion. I've heard of straight hair growing in curly after it's been shaved off for surgery or lost during an illness. You have curly sex glands, maybe, I told myself.

I heard Dottie come in next door and I sat up to dress for dinner.

My bafflement was as great as ever. I had only to picture the penetrating blue eyes, the look of private sorrow, to know there was more to Greggan's bitterness than I could guess.

And then I remembered Lady Fanquill's esoteric counsel: "Remember he is not unkind . . . even though he has had his share of unkindness . . ."

II. . . .

I was thankful for the hubbub in the dining room created by the grouse shooters, jubilant after their day of blasting on the moors, followed by their hour of imbibing in the bar. Americans abroad may have a reputation for being loud, but a roomful of American sportsmen couldn't have been noisier than these Sassenachs, or Southerners, as the Scots call the English. On the best of terms we three women would have found it hard to make conversation over their uproar.

We were a little on edge tonight. Lilah's practice drive and Dottie's immediately following suit had brought close to the surface an as yet undeclared rivalry between them. As a result we were extra-careful to avoid dangerous ground, and what conversation we were able to exchange was stilted.

But as usual Jock, with eyes in the back of his head, came to jolly us. "Doctors prescribe it," he said, deftly conveying a diapered bottle from place to place. "A day of fresh Scottish air to be followed by two glasses of wine at dinner. You mustn't try to get by on air alone, it just won't do." He left us smiling.

I remembered he was a distant cousin of the laird. A family business, he'd told me. Severn, too, with his aristocratic symptoms, must be kindred. They all had the family hair, with a touch of gold in it. Munro was no doubt an old castle retainer. Dougal the gamekeeper with his craggy face looked as if he'd grown out of the rock of the surrounding hills.

Presumably it would benefit all of them, if only indirectly, when the MacLarkie land reverted to Strathburne. I wondered if they all knew the terms of Bart's will.

"What did Colin have to say?" Lilah broke in on my thoughts. She looked matronly but very nice in a powder-blue knit which set off her pale fine hair. I realized her curiosity was mixed with misgiving. She disapproved of Colin, as any fairly straight-laced person would; as I do myself at times.

"Do you know, I never opened the letter! I lay down for a rest and forgot it. I'll fetch it after dinner."

"Colin's your husband's younger brother, right?" asked Dottie.

I nodded. "The sole survivor. He's the maverick of the family, the only one with artistic talent. He does special effects for television shows, in Burbank."

"When he chooses to work," put in Lilah.

I grinned. "Yes, he's a carefree one, isn't he?" I continued to Dottie, "You met him at Bart's memorial service, remember?" I attended the service in a wheelchair, convoyed by Dottie. "He came to the house afterward with the rest of the crowd."

"I remember. Black hair, white teeth, gold

chains around his neck. A swinger, right? Not like your husband, I gather."

Lilah hooted.

"No," I said, "not in the least. But we got along well together." Even when Colin imagined, or pretended, he was in love with me. "You can't help liking him."

"I can help liking him," said Lilah.

I looked for the telltale lines of humor at the corners of her mouth but I didn't find them. "Maybe because you saw even less of him than I did, darling." And I explained to Dottie, "He lived in an entirely different world from Bart's and mine."

Lilah had her moment of triumph then. She looked at me with a soft little smile. "I guess you didn't notice," she told me. "Colin's letter had an English stamp on it."

I met Lady Fanquill at the foot of the staircase as I went up to fetch the letter. In mauve and dove-gray chiffon with trailing tiers and panels, a beautiful dress that might have been made by Paquin in the twenties, she looked like a sea anemone gently stirred by the tide.

"They are rather obscene, are they not?" she said. "I have never admired men who derive such gross stimulation from killing birds and animals."

Clinging to separate banisters, we slowly mounted the stairs together. She was referring, of course, to the noisy grouse hunters. "Better though," I answered, "than hacking away at each other with poleaxes."

"Ah, but they have only to press a button to destroy half the world. I hope he was not rude?"

Now I could only look nonplussed.

"Jean told me you had gone looking for him," said Lady Fanquill, by way of clarification.

Ah: her nephew again. I decided not to beat about the bush. "Yes, in a way, he was rude."

"There, you see? I imagined he might be. I tried to warn you."

"You told me," I reminded her, hoping she would elucidate, however obliquely, "he'd had his share of unkindness."

"And so he has." She studied me for an instant with her pale, unreadable eyes. We had come to the top of the first flight of steps where the staircase divides right and left, and we paused there. She said, "You have had your share also, have you not, my dear?"

"Not of unkindness, no. Unless you want to call it the unkindness of fate."

"My dear, I do not believe in fate at all. Fate is man's invention, to excuse his own folly. How odd, to philosophize on a stair landing. We must go our separate ways.

He will not be happy if he has been rude, you will see. Good night."

She turned and ascended lightly toward her corridor.

III. . . .

Hello, Sue-love! Colin began characteristically, scrawling with a green felt-tip pen on lined yellow legal paper. I read the letter aloud to Lilah and Dottie in the lounge after coffee. The grouse shooters, facing an early rise next morning, were scattering to their rooms. Major Barsington-Banks had leaned forward confidentially to us to say, "Rum!" and taken his great sleepy-faced lady off to bed.

We used to have a family expression, Bart and I: "Well, that's Colin." It meant that Colin, the only one of the brothers to break out of the conservative MacLarkie mold, had to be accepted on his own terms. He would drop by our hilltop house fairly frequently for a spell, wearing his high-priced denims and partially tinted glasses, his hair tousled or carefully "styled" according to his whim; and then we might not see him again for months. Despite his proclaimed ardor for me, we were never quite sure what his sexual inclinations actually were, but they didn't concern us. The important thing about Colin was that, however outrageous, his

70

company was always enjoyable. However undependable, he had undeniable sweetness. He loved luxury and he owed Bart quite a lot of money; I suspect his more closely spaced visits had to do with his being temporarily hard up, but, well, that was Colin, and after Bart's death I wrote off the debt which Bart, the level-headed, had kept account of.

A black sheep to some extent, I suppose, but both Bart and I, I do believe, had moments of envying Colin.

Am staying with a friend in London, I read. This in fact didn't surprise me. Colin's crowd are always on the move, in and out of each other's apartments, in and out of relationships, in and out of jobs, in and out of far-flung countries.

Just wouldn't be right to miss the chance to see you while I'm so near, would it? Actually, Sue-love, I long to know if my prayers for you have been answered and if you're once more your old ravishing self. Lilah's with you, isn't she? Implore her to put up with me for a few days and tell her I promise to be on my best behavior. Forgive the scribble — Laurie's flat so teems with drop-ins and drop-outs that there's no private place to write except the loo. There, darling, if you've no violent objections I'll come along to the castle on my way back to the States. Ta, love, and kisses. Colin.

I put down the letter with a shake of the head, laughing at the same time. How like him, throwing in British slang and leaving out his arrival date. I didn't know who Laurie was, whether male or female, and there was no return address.

Then I saw Lilah's face and my laughter died.

"He can't," she breathed, as though the thought gave her pain.

"He can, Lilah, and he undoubtedly will." I spoke softly and pacifyingly. I knew she didn't care for Colin but I had no idea she felt so strongly about him. "It's only for a few days."

"The nerve, Sue! The incredible nerve!"

Dottie watched her guardedly, saying nothing.

"But, Lilah, he's Bart's brother. I have no choice."

"He leaves you no choice!"

"He's always fun, Lilah. He'll liven us up." Our tricky threesome, I was beginning to think, needed an addition.

Lilah gathered up glasses, purse, needlepoint, and shawl. "I don't need livening up, not by Colin. But if you can stand it then I suppose I must. But, Susan, the less you see of Colin, now that Bart is gone, the better. I don't trust him and I never have. Good night."

Dottie and I sat in silence for a few minutes

after Lilah's departure. We were alone in the shadowed room. I was grateful to Dottie for not making one of her wisecracks. She swung her foot in its navy-blue tie-shoe. She was wearing a long Hawaiian skirt of large yellow and orange blossoms, a shocking pink sweater-top, and a wool stole in the tartan of Hunting Stewart.

"Which of you is right?" she said.

"About Colin? I don't know. Let me put it this way: Colin likes people to think he's casual, nonchalant, and amoral. But I'm certain that's to disguise a very kind, thoughtful, moral person. He's always broke, and I think one of the reasons is that he's always giving someone the shirt off his back."

Dottie's foot still bobbed up and down. "Good," she said. "I think you need a friend like that." I was about to demand an explanation but she spoke again. "I gotta ask you something." She wrapped her stole closer and sat with her shoulders hunched, although we were close to the fire. "I've got my reasons. I know you have the usual amnesia about the time before the accident, but you do know you were going to a cocktail party. Do you remember who was there, at your house, that day?"

"For heaven's sake, Dottie, what are you getting at?"

"Just answer me if you can. Who was there at the house besides you and Bart?"

I shook my head at her, mystified. "Well, Angela and Rafael, of course, and I guess Joe, the gardener. No, it was Sunday, wasn't it, so – "

"I don't mean the servants. I mean guests. Relatives, even. People who stopped by. Who had *been* there?"

"I don't remember! Dottie, really! The accident blotted out everything that preceded it. The day just – disappeared from my mind."

"Was Lilah there?"

"I don't remember! I don't want to remember! What difference does it make? It's a *blessing* not to remember. Dottie, will you please tell me – "

"Okay, okay, forget it." Dottie was suddenly on her feet. "You know me, I'm not satisfied till I get everything straight in my head." Then unthinkingly she contradicted herself. "I just wanted to see if your memory is coming back. Wanta come up now, hon'?" Without covering her mouth she gave way to a prodigious yawn, and in the middle of it started talking, down through the scale. "I took the air and the two glasses of wine and they work. Boy, I'm just about knocked out. C'mon, lemme see you get up outa that chair without your crutch."

Automatically I obeyed, and in the effort forgot what I wanted to say to her.

Now, late at night, I remember. The wind buffets my window, which opens outward on a brass arm, and clouds fly across a three-quarter moon. I awoke thinking I heard someone at my door, whether the one into Dottie's room or the one into the hall I couldn't tell. I put on my bedside light and watched the door handles but they didn't move. There must be a draft through the corridor.

I take up my notebook and set down the forgotten protest. But I have friends, I'd been going to say to Dottie. I have you and Lilah! I listen again. No, all is quiet.

Dottie's questions stirred up something in me, as if it had been lying there undisturbed, still as the sediment in an old bottle of wine, for a long time. She shook me, and muddy particles rose to fly nervously about, creating a sensation like quivering. And alone in my room with the vast sleeping castle around me, I ask again: Haven't I? Haven't I friends?

Was she trying to tell me I have an enemy?

CHAPTER 5

I. . . .

"You still want to go to Kirkangus?" Dottie asked doubtfully. She had just finished giving me a lesson in getting in and out of the tub by myself.

The change of wind in the night produced a raw damp day. Mists coiled over the loch, and everything had turned the nebulous color of jade. The laird in his skiff was not to be seen. Shifting tiers of cloud draped the hills.

"We might as well, Dottie. We're all agreed we need to bestir ourselves and get out of the castle."

She didn't answer for a moment. At once I felt the inner depths she had shaken last night becoming unsettled again. Dottie closemouthed is a lot more disquieting than Dottie outspoken.

"Yeah," she said at last, "we do. Okay, let's run through the tub routine again."

"Oh, come on, Dottie —"

"*Do* it. No, now be sure everything's in place

76

before you start. Okay, siddown. Swing your legs in. Atta girl. Hang onto that grip. Great. Now out again. You got it!" She gave me a big heated towel. "That's another step forward. I'll leave you to dress. Bundle up, it's colder out than yesterday."

"Yes, boss. You're cutting your own throat, you know. You'll get me to the point where I won't need you." It was the kind of banter we'd always indulged in, but the recollection of Lilah's cautioning words about possessive nurses made me redden suddenly.

There was the merest pause in Dottie's walk and then she said breezily over her shoulder, "That's what I gotta aim for, kiddo." She didn't see my blush.

Clothed in wool dress, scarf, and fur-lined raincoat, I left the room before Dottie was ready, went downstairs and looked in the bar for Jock. The bar was empty. No one was about in the lounge either. Ashes smoldered in the hearth, and a vacuum cleaner whined in the dining room. I could hear Jean dealing on the phone with someone who wanted a reservation, and remembering I had to speak to her about Colin's proposed arrival, I sat down in the lounge near the hall door to wait until she'd finished.

Her caller evidently wished insistently to

come late in the deer-stalking season, and Jean was explaining with infinite patience that the hotel was not open after the middle of October. She hung up at last and then I heard Jock's voice.

"One of these days, darling lass, you're going to blow your top. I hope I'm around to witness it."

"Be careful," she answered. "You might be." Her voice was muffled as though she was bent over one of her ledgers.

"Oho," said Jock, "I might be in the line of fire?"

"You might even be the target."

I'd have made my presence known if I'd thought they were engaged in anything but casual talk, very nearly like passing the time of day. I felt they'd break off at any moment.

"Jean, Jean, have ye no pity for me?"

"Pity for you, my darling lad? Very little."

"I'd rather you lose your temper with me than show such heartless indifference."

"Very well, Gordon, I *shall* lose my temper with you, I promise, but not this morning, please, I'm far too busy."

"Ye'll drive me to drink. 'What's happened to Jocko?' people will ask. 'He's taken to cryin' in his beer.' And those in the know will answer, 'Och, it's a shame, and him sae young. He has a bad case of dampened ardor.' "

"Ha ha. The day your ardor is dampened, Jocko, is the day I sprout wings and fly."

"Jean, Jean, if I thought you'd take me seriously for one moment I'd kiss the rest of the world good-bye."

"Jocko, you could no more stop kissing than I could take you seriously. Now do go away while I wrestle with my books. Our season is ending and there are all the bills to be made out."

"All right, I'm off to the bar to commence drowning my sorrow."

"Cheers," she said, absentmindedly.

I heard the swinging door moan as he went into the service corridor; from there he would take a rear door into the bar without having to traverse the lounge.

I got up and instead of turning into the hall, went back to the bar by way of the lounge.

It's a small paneled room, cozy in the evening with a diminutive hearth fire, but in the morning dark, chilly, and sour-smelling. Jock, not in the least dejected, was briskly setting up for the day, unlocking cupboards and extracting bottles, his jacket off and a striped apron over his red vest.

At sight of me he put down his bottles, pulled the tea towel off his shoulder and faced me with both hands on the polished wood. "Mrs.

79

MacLarkie, good morning! What can I do for you?" And he wore the face of the professional bartender, prepared without moral judgment to satisfy one's thirst no matter what the time of day.

"I only need a bit of information, Jock. We're driving in to Kirkangus."

His face relaxed. "I couldn't believe you were about to order a pick-me-up. How can I inform you?"

"You live in Kirkangus, don't you? Is there a place where we can have lunch?"

"That's all too easy. The Angus Arms Hotel."

"Thank you. It sounds very nice."

"Well, it's not, to tell you the truth. It was built in the 1890s for commercial travelers of irreproachable Calvinist principles. Need I say more? But it's the only place in Kirkangus to find a half-decent meal. Ask Jean to ring them up and reserve the small room and tell them to light the fire. Do not order mutton. Ask for an omelette, or take the fish. Be prepared in any case for a taste of true Scottish austerity."

I had to smile. He sounded as if he were instructing someone about to explore the native quarter of a dangerous city. And once again, when I smiled, he fell into a trancelike gaze. I thought I looked about as sexy as Queen Elizabeth when she is dressed for the rain with a scarf over her head. Nevertheless he took on the rather stunned, apprehensive, speculative expression he wore on the bridge the other day, only this time it didn't catch him in the middle of a sentence.

I said, "You don't live at the Angus Arms yourself?"

And once more he pulled himself together. He gazed at me sadly. "I would not meet their rigorous standards." He dropped his eyes with becoming modesty. "I am the traditionally wayward son of a minister. My dad hopes someday I'll see the light. I live, believe it or not, at the manse."

"Doesn't that cramp your style?"

He looked up, still solemn. "Not in the least."

I didn't think it best to pursue the subject. "There's one more thing I'd like to know." And this, I didn't tell him, was the real reason why I was there.

"You have only to ask." He looked exceedingly worshipful.

But I'm not really good at subterfuge so I had to go at it rather flat-footedly. "The wife of an earl is a countess, isn't she?"

"She is." With a tiny flicker his eyes were almost imperceptibly wary.

"Then where is the Countess of Strathburne?"

The eyes didn't waver, but at once the face took on the accommodating mask he wears in the dining room. "I believe she lives most of the time on the Continent."

"They're divorced?"

"They are." He still smiled, but he drew back and began to polish the gleaming surface of the bar with his tea towel.

It's a family business, this hotel and the laird's divorce is a family affair. I was pretty sure I would draw nothing more out of Gordon Thornhill. "I know it's none of my business," I tried to explain, "but it's the kind of question a hotel guest might ask, seeing a solitary earl about the place with a grown daughter. Especially a guest whom the laird has fished out of the loch." I drew away. "Especially a *nosy* guest."

"Och, no." He leaned toward me again, his voice lowered. "You're not the first to ask. But it was an unpleasant divorce, you see, a blow to a man's pride, and the London press ate it up, so it's what might be called a sore subject."

I was conscience-stricken. "It happened recently?"

"No, no. Six or seven years ago."

I shook my head. If it happened seven years ago and was still a sore subject, it must have been very unpleasant indeed. I thought Jock was about to say something more, as Jean had been, taking in a breath with the words on the tip of his tongue, but he thought better of it and closed his lips and that was that.

I gave the bar-top a soft conclusive pat. "My friends will be waiting for me. Thank you for your advice, Jock."

His hand came down softly on mine. "There is nothing I would refuse you, were it within my power to grant it."

His voice had a deep vibrato of emotion, but he still wore a faint smile, both quizzical and penitent, and I looked into his appealing eyes, a greener shade of the family blue, and was once more tempted to meet him halfway. He is a charming fellow without question, elegant and nimble-witted, and no doubt a proficient lover. His barely disguised proposition came when my ego needed a boost, after having been set down by the laird, and when my glands were growing in curly. His hand on mine was warm and full of promise.

But I have no experience in the art of not getting into a love affair too deeply, and I'd concluded from his conversation with Jean, if I hadn't guessed it already, that Gordon Thornhill has. An affair of no lasting involvement might have been just the ticket; possibly Dr. Kohl would have given it his approval, but I wasn't sure I could successfully carry off my part of it. On top of everything, instinct told me he was meant for Jean and Jean for him, provided their eyes could be opened to each other. If Gordon married Jean, he would become in a sense the earl's heir and the castle and the land would eventually be his. A tidy family tie-up.

"You are a dear, Gordon," I told him, gently withdrawing my hand from under his. A look of penitence may have filled my own eyes. "But you see, I still have to be very careful about every step I take, and there really isn't much I can ask of anyone yet." It was a random reply but he seemed to understand me.

"Aye, then," he said, straightening, not a whit downcast, and he let me go.

Yet I'd no sooner left the bar than I began wondering what it was he'd been on the point of telling me about the laird.

"A terrible blow to a man's pride" implied cuckoldry. "An unpleasant divorce" sounded as if a corespondent had been named, and if "the London press ate it up" it must have involved a corespondent of note or of wealth or both, for I didn't believe the London press would necessarily eat up the domestic tribulations of an impecunious, out-of-the-way laird. Moreoever, "living on the Continent" suggested tax-dodging affluence.

Alas for Greggan of Strathburne. He'd not only had to make do with a depleted estate but he'd lost a wife as well. I felt I was a little closer to the origins of his misogyny.

Nevertheless, though I felt more compassion for him today than yesterday, I couldn't see why he had to take out his resentment on me.

II. . . .

I stood fighting panic. It rose in waves from my lungs into my shoulders and arms and flooded downward through my bowels to the soles of my feet . . . *"The brakes, Susan! We've got no brakes!"* . . . And I tried to hold back, to stop the weightless plunge through the air, and the earth spun far below . . .

Dottie's voice said, "I think we'd better not go."

"Och, the mists are nae so bad. Ye hae nothing to fear so long as ye're home by dark."

In particles, chaos settled, became order, thinned away. I was in the courtyard. Munro was holding the door handle of our car, waiting to open it for us. Dottie had slipped her arm through mine to grip my wrist. Lilah watched me, her face troubled.

"No," I said. "We'll go. I want to go. I've just got to get over this."

"Okay, kiddo, if you say so. You do have to

get over it, and I guess this is the only way. In fact, I'd like to see you start driving again yourself. Okay, let's go. I'll drive real slow."

"But Susan said —" Lilah began on a plaintive note, and stopped. I gave her a little pleading shake of the head. She let out her breath, then helped me into the back seat, which I prefer, and climbed in beside Dottie without another word.

We crept out through the great gate and down the ramp and over the bridge to the loch-road, where we turned right. It was little more than a paved lane along the shore, with just enough room for two small cars to pass, and at the moment there was no traffic at all. Dottie's careful pace made it seem as if we were out for a stroll. My moist hands unclenched. I looked up the steep green closely cropped swards on our left into stands of firs and black crags with burns spilling down among them, until they disappeared into the lowering clouds. On our right, brown boulders made a border between us and the loch where the dull waters splashed in the wind, only a little below the level of the road.

I was in control of myself even when we left the loch and began to climb toward the pass, rising into ghostly, drifting shrouds of mist. We were hemmed in now by towering firs and there were no precipitious drops to terrify me. Dottie drove steadily and surely.

We leveled off at last in a high forsaken world of mauve-colored heather and rusty grass, a long empty moor close under the clouds, its borders vanishing into what must be still higher hills. Only a few sheep wandered here, lifting their black faces from the grass to stare at us unconcernedly with their strange pale-yellow eyes.

"Oh, it's wild, isn't it," breathed Lilah, thrilled in spite of herself.

"Not a beer can in sight," said Dottie. "I must say this for the Scotch, they're neat and tidy."

"The Scots, Dottie," I told her. "Scotch is a whiskey."

"Izzat so," said Dottie. She can take corrections or leave them alone.

We were on a one-track road, with passing bays every fifty yards or so. We had come this way from Glasgow, too exhausted to take in our surroundings, but I remembered the system of passing: when a car approached, one or the other of us pulled into the nearest bay, signaling "You first!" with our headlights, and as we came alongside, the driver raised a finger or two in salute. A typically thrifty, typically courteous arrangement. Today we passed no one, and after traversing several miles of moor we arrived at a signpost pointing east to Inverness and south to Kirkangus, where Dottie came to a full stop.

"Okay, how do you feel, Sue?"

"I'm all right now."

"I'm not crazy about this fog. I wouldn't like to see it get worse. There's no reason why we can't turn around and go back, and start out again tomorrow."

"After coming all this way?" asked Lilah. "It doesn't scare *me*."

"I'm asking Susan."

"The sign says eleven miles to Kirkangus," I said. "It must be about the same distance back to the castle. Munro didn't think it would get worse. Why don't we go on? If it's okay with you, it is with me."

For answer Dottie shifted into drive again and we made the turn, heading downhill to Kirkangus.

It ranged alongside a stream, a neat town of gray stone houses brightened by riotous rose and dahlia gardens. The shops were closed for lunch and there were few pedestrians about. The Angus Arms Hotel, also of gray granite, with sharp bleak angles, rose prominently halfway down the High Street.

The inside was of the same bleak order, highly varnished and chilly. An elderly maid conducted us silently to a stark chamber where three places had been set for us at one end of a long table, its linen starched to the consistency of cardboard. Over the fireplace hung a steel engraving of a stag on a barren Highland peak, and below in the hearth glowed a tiny electric heater which had little effect on the temperature of the room.

We made the best of it, speaking in whispers, working our way through fish and brussels sprouts and the usual two kinds of potatoes, boiled and fried. When Dottie asked for the salt in a sepulchral voice we all three went into fits of surreptitious giggles.

On our way out I inquired at the desk about a solicitor and was directed to Archibald Mac-Baine of MacBaine and Atherton, on the High Street. I'd avoided asking for this information at the castle, so as not to arouse curiosity; I'd become sensitive about the MacLarkie land.

Dottie planned to shop for postcards and souvenirs. "You wanta come too, Lilah?"

"Thanks, Dottie, I'll tag along with Susan." Dottie left us and we set off down the High Street, busier now that the shops were open. "You don't mind, do you, Susan? Dottie really doesn't want my company, although it was nice of her to ask me." She made a little grimace. "Or maybe she just didn't want me to go with you."

I stifled a little sigh. "Now, Lilah."

"You're going to a lawyer. You're not going to sign anything over to her, are you?"

"No, Lilah, I am not." I took her by the arm. "I wish you'd get that conniving-nurse idea out of your head."

"I wish I would, too. I want to. But look, you'll have to admit, she doesn't like us being alone together."

"I don't have to admit any such thing."

"For some reason she doesn't trust me. Or," she added, before I could interrupt, "She doesn't want *you* to trust me."

I was about to remonstrate, when we found ourselves abreast of the MacBaine and Atherton brass doorplate, so assiduously polished that the script had faded into the metal.

"Here we are," I said, relieved. "Do you want to come in and wait for me? And, please, Lilah, try having a little more trust, yourself."

"If I had more," she said quietly, "I probably wouldn't be here."

I gave her a quick stare. But I didn't ask her what she meant; I refused to dwell on the matter any longer.

I pushed open the door.

III. . . .

We stepped into a tiny vestibule, its highly

90

waxed floor uneven, its paneling painted black and white, its odor of another century; and then, obeying gilt-lettered instructions, we opened a glass-paneled door on our left and entered a hushed librarylike room where two or three clerks worked in silence at mahogany desks. No clatter of typewriters, no jangle of telephones; only a single preoccupied cough.

An elderly man with a teenaged complexion rose and came forward to inquire if he might serve me. It wasn't the sort of place one ought to drop in on off the street, I thought; I should have written a formal letter requesting an appointment. But being American obviates a lot of explanations, and I stated my name and asked if I might see Mr. Archibald MacBaine. Neither was it the sort of place where one was made to feel insignificant, and the old man bowed graciously and departed with my petition.

In a few moments he returned to say Mr. MacBaine would be pleased to see me. I knew Lilah was ready to accompany me, but hardheartedly I told her I wouldn't be long, and she sat down to wait in the black and white hall.

Step by step I hoisted myself up the little flight of stairs in the wake of the elderly clerk, and was ushered into a tall-windowed room overlooking a rear garden.

"Mrs. Barton MacLarkie," enunciated the clerk clearly, and bowed himself out.

A small roly-poly man in furry brown Harris tweed came bounding forward to shake my hand, his smile radiant and merry, his skin shining — eyelids, nostrils, ears, all agleam and all of a piece with the shining doorplate and waxed floors. He had thin clean brown hair parted in the middle and a brownish cast to his gleaming skin, and his brown eyes were full of dancing lights. He hastened to draw up a chair by his desk, settled me in it, skipped to his own aged leather chair, plumped down in it, placing a hand on each furry knee as if prepared to leap to his feet at an instant's notice, and said, "Noo then, Mrs. MacLarkie!"

At once I was convinced one could have nothing but the most equitable dealings with him. Catching my breath after this whirlwind welcome, I explained that I'd inherited some land and wished to take whatever legal steps were necessary to claim it, and I handed over my documents. He donned a pair of gold-rimmed spectacles, perfectly round, and perused the papers carefully, smiling and nodding, "Aye, aye," approvingly. Then he put the documents aside and lucidly spelled out the procedure for confirming my right of ownership and placing it on record.

Would he undertake this procedure on my behalf, I asked him. Cair-tainly! He would be happy to do so! Perhaps, I suggested, someone at the castle could show me the land if he would have a map drawn up. He would see to it!

"There is one more thing, Mr. MacBaine, something of a more personal nature."

He sat up watchfully, like an alert little brown owl, the dancing eyes steadying ever so slightly.

"My husband's grandfather lived somewhere in this area before emigrating to the States. Of course that was long before your time, but I wonder if you happen to know: was he, and is he still, resented here? Was there bad blood between him and the then-laird of Strathburne before he emigrated? Could he have purchased the land by ruse, through an intermediary . . . ?" My voice dwindled.

It was plain to see that Mr. Archibald Mac-Baine was not all chuckles and jollity. His brown eyes, as expressionless now as agate in his beaming face, must have put an end to a lot of hapless gabbling, like mine, in his years of practice.

"It was a very long time ago," he murmured, not moving a muscle.

"Yes," I murmured back. "I was hoping you might enlighten me." I was certain at this moment that he could, if he chose; only he did not choose. "I realize it's not exactly a matter to take up with a solicitor, but since the land is mine to keep or dispose of, I would appreciate knowing whatever is pertinent to it, even though it's hearsay." Pretty good, I told myself; you sound like an upstanding, legal-minded gossipmonger. *Very* good, that tempting bit about disposal.

But Archibald MacBaine did not rise to the bait. His level gaze stonewalled me. "Hearsay is well-known to be unreliable, Mrs. MacLarkie. I let it pass in one ear and r-r-rapidly out the other, lest I be influenced by it. I should not like to think you'd be burdened by it either."

"Burdened, Mr. MacBaine?"

A spark in his eye commended me for sharpness. "Aye, my lady. Whatever your husband's grandfather may or may not have done, it is at rest in the past."

I was about to contradict him but I thought better of it. What was the use? He wasn't going to give.

He bounded to his feet as I rose, all vivacity again, and pumped my hand. He would attend to my requirements at once. He trotted alongside me to the door. "Allow me to help you down to the street!" he cried. I told him my sister-in-law was waiting in the hall. "I bid you good day then, Mrs. MacLarkie. You will hear from me shortly!" We parted on the landing.

Whatever Grandfather MacLarkie had or had not done, it was not at rest in the past. And I was pretty sure that whatever went into one of the shining ears of Mr. Archibald MacBaine did not so rapidly go out the other again.

"Wait, Sue!" Lilah started up the stairs. "The steps are very steep. Let me help you!"

The street door opened below and Dottie came in. She took in the situation in a split second. "No!" she cried. "Don't touch her!" Halfway up the stairs, Lilah froze. "Let her come down by herself. C'mon, Sue-baby, you can make it."

"Of course I can," I said. "But thanks anyway, Lilah."

And Lilah looked at me with her lips pursed, as if to say, You see what I mean about Dottie?

IV. . . .

The car was parked outside. Dottie had brought it around.

"Now may I drive?" demanded Lilah.

I could see she was ready to lock horns. "Yes," I said quickly. "Dottie, I did promise."

"You may not know it," Lilah informed her, "but I drove for the Red Cross for years, didn't I, Sue?"

"You did, darling."

Dottie gave me a look combining protest and resignation, and gave over to Lilah.

Would it have been any different if Dottie had driven, and not Lilah? That is the terrifying question.

The mist closed down on us as we climbed out of Kirkangus. Lilah slowed to a crawl and turned on the headlights. No one spoke. It was no time for arguing. I have been in worse California fogs, but not on a one-track road in an alien wilderness.

"I'm going to sound the horn," said Lilah. "We ought to be getting near the crossroad where we turn for the castle."

It sounded like a bicycle horn but it was penetrating. We went beeping up the long slope to the moor, fully aware that someone might be headed toward us just as blindly.

It began to seem as if we should long ago have reached the crossroad. "We couldn't have missed it, could we?" I asked.

"Not possibly."

"I don't like this one iota," said Dottie.

"Well, neither do I," snapped Lilah. We were all on edge. "Wouldn't it be a good idea if I pulled into one of these bays and stopped? Maybe the mist will lift if we wait a few minutes. It was very patchy this morning, remember?" Dottie and I agreed, and Lilah pulled off the road.

She switched off the ignition and an eerie silence descended on us, enveloping us. I could hear my ears ringing. The mist was white as milk. Ghostly shifting shapes and ominous vistas appeared and vanished.

"I'm going to walk up the road a little way and see if the signpost is up ahead," said Lilah suddenly. "I won't go far."

We were too oppressed to say yes or no. She disappeared at once. The smell of damp inside the car was dispiriting. I closed my eyes.

I heard the car door open. Dottie said, "I'm not going after her, don't worry, but I don't think she should have gone off alone like that." When she was outside the car, her hand still on the door handle, she yelled, "*Li*-lah! Li-*lah*? You all right?"

I thought I heard a faint answer. Then before I was aware of it myself, Dottie shrieked, "Jesus God, the car's moving!"

It was rolling backward, very slowly. Dottie tore open the car door and flung herself across the passenger seat. She had to scramble about then to right herself and stretch her foot to the brake. It seemed to take forever. I was leaning forward, gripping the sides of the driver's seat in front of me, looking backward as the car seemed to gain momentum.

Dottie brought the car to a jerking halt before it left the bay; it couldn't have traveled more than ten feet. Dottie coiled herself into the driver's seat, groaned, leaned her elbow on the windowsill, and as though not trusting herself to speak, stared out the window.

In the next moment Lilah reappeared, all smiles. She apparently didn't notice the car had moved. "It's right up the road! We're not a hundred feet from it!"

Dottie folded her arms. "D'you know what happened to us? What nearly happened?"

"No," gasped Lilah, startled, "what?"

"We nearly rolled backward down the hill."

"Oh, *no!* But I left the handbrake on!"

"Well, the handbrake didn't hold. And I don't care if you drove for the Teamster's Union, I'm taking the car home. Understand? Get in. Let's go."

Lilah marched around the car and got in. "For Susan's sake," she said, "I will do as you say. But I do *not* like being ordered about in that tone of voice. It was *not* my fault that the —"

"Stop it," I cried. The accumulated tension was more than I could bear. "Stop it, both of you! I won't have any more of it. If we can't get along together we'll have to pack up and go home, all three of us!"

For a moment neither of them spoke.

Dottie gave a great sigh. She turned and patted my hand. "Poor Sue. You've had it with us and I don't blame you." Quietly Lilah began to cry, covering her face with her hands. "Three's a crowd, like always," Dottie continued. "You get three women together, two of them are gonna wind up on the outs." I thought for a frightened moment that Dottie was going to bow out, and then I wondered if I *was* dependent on her, at least psychologically, even after I'd become more independent physically. "So any day now Colin arrives," she went on, "and maybe things will ease up. At least we'll have four for bridge, right? Meanwhile I'll try and keep my big mouth shut and stay outa Lilah's hair. How's that?"

In a choked voiced Lilah said, "I think you owe me an apology!"

"I d'know what for, but I apologize."

"All right, let's try it and see," I pleaded. I touched Lilah's shoulder. "Cheer up, darling. We'll all try."

"If that's what you want, Susan." Lilah blew her nose, patted her hair, and set her lips tightly together. Dottie started the car.

The mist, we discovered, had miraculously lifted. The signpost was just ahead of us.

I was thankful. I sat back and closed my eyes

again. I wanted only to get back to the castle.

V. . . .

Dottie came to my room at bedtime as usual to give me my nightly temperature and blood pressure check, more a matter of routine now than a necessity. I got into bed and she sat on at my dressing table, picking things up and putting them down again, and for a while we talked about changing my exercises, cutting out some of them and concentrating more on others.

She clasped her hands between her knees. "You know, you could get along without me now. I guess we both know that." She unclasped her hands and folded her arms. "But I'll tell you sump'm, Sue-baby: if you think I'm going to leave you alone here with Lilah, you got another think coming." She drew her shoulders up as if she were cold. "Over my dead body!"

"Dottie, for heaven's sake!"

"Yeah, maybe I'm paranoid. Maybe I'm way out in left field. But I gotta get this off my chest." First Lilah, I thought, and now Dottie. "She was trying to get into your room last night."

I remembered the rattle that wakened me. "There's nothing so terrible about that, is there?"

"Sue, it was the *way* she was trying to get in,

100

turning the door handle very, very slowly—"

"She didn't want to disturb me in case I was asleep!"

"No, lemme finish. You know I sleep with my ears awake, but this was more of a feeling. I got out of bed and looked in the hall, and she was very flustered when I asked her what she wanted. She said, 'I wanted to borrow an aspirin.' I didn't believe her. She knows I have headaches and she knows I always have aspirin on hand. It would have made more sense if she'd knocked on *my* door."

"She probably wanted to see me without rousing you." I could hear Lilah saying, She seems to *guard* you from me. "You probably scared her out of her wits and she said the first thing that came into her head."

"I don't think she scares that easy. I think under that timid act she's made of steel."

I thought so, too, only I called it stout-hearted.

"Anyway," Dottie went on, "I got her an aspirin out of my medicine chest and she went back to bed. But this morning, after she went downstairs, I went into her room. I used my own key on her door, the locks are all the same, the old-fashioned kind; anybody can get into anybody's room if they want to. I know, it was sneaky, but I had to satisfy myself. I went into her bathroom, and sure enough, she's *got* a bottle of aspirin."

"Dottie." We were both whispering. "You're implying she was up to no good. For God's sake, what would Lilah be up to?"

Dottie hesitated. She got to her feet. "Maybe we better leave it that I'm paranoid." She crossed the room to my door. "Keep your door locked with the key turned in the lock, like this, see? That way only a professional could open the door without making a noise." She moved to our connecting door. "I'm sorry if I upset you, Sue, but I had to pass along to you what I been thinking. I want your eyes to be open."

"Dottie, you have not passed along to me what you've been thinking, not all of it, I know you haven't." I could hear Lilah saying, She doesn't want you to trust me. "You might as well tell me. I know I'm going to hate it, whatever it is, but we might as well have it all out as long as we've gone this far."

She stood at the door, an incongruous figure in her flamboyant colors, hands on hips, pivoting on one out-thrust heel. And in those few seconds, while she made up her mind, I half-guessed what was coming as if I'd known it all along.

"Kiddo," she said softly, "I been on this case a long while, and certain little things have been adding up." Her eyes lifted to mine from across the room. "There've just been too many accidents. Hasn't it ever occurred to you they might not've *been* accidents?"

CHAPTER 6

I. . . .

Everything comes to a halt, they say, on a
Scottish Sabbath. Even the view from my window was a picture of suspended animation, the
sky a uniform milky overcast, the loch a dark
mirror again, reflecting darkened hills.

Dottie drove off early to Mass in Inverness, a
good forty miles, and Lilah was nowhere in
evidence. Probably she'd found a secluded corner to do her needlework — she's on the fifth
chair-seat. There are plenty of curtained window seats, alcoves, and anterooms in the castle
in which to be alone.

Shooting, too, is suspended on Sunday, but in
fact most of the grouse shooters left over the
weekend. Only the Barsington-Bankses and a
few nonsporting English guests occupied the
lounge, reading the Sunday papers in isolated
groups, so utterly silent that blindfolded you'd
swear the room was empty.

Miss Pinwherry, Jean's substitute, had taken

over the reception desk, and Munro and Severn were stowing luggage in the car of a departing grouse shooter, so I set out for a walk without the customary friendly send-off.

For a while I walked with my shoulders hunched and my eyes on the ground. I felt depressed, yet I couldn't let myself think why. If I once gave way to serious consideration of Dottie's suspicions of steel-fibered Lilah, or Lilah's suspicions of paranoid, possessive Dottie, I'd release irretrievable demons. I couldn't even consider the so-called accidents, whether they were all bona fide, or some bona fide and one not, or one bona fide and some not, or whether they had been caused by the same or different persons. I don't think it's that I haven't the courage to face facts, or that I don't trust Dottie, or Lilah. But something warns me not to embark on a path of thought from which I might never be able to turn back.

I hoped frivolous, warmhearted Colin would turn up soon. Yet it wouldn't be unlike him, I thought, not to turn up at all.

The length of the loch-road seemed longer, of course, on foot than in the car, and after trudging nearly half a mile I was beginning to tire. I found a flat-topped boulder on the water's edge for a resting place. A car or two passed at first and then I was quite alone between the mirrorlike loch on one side and the steep green flanks of the hills on the other.

I was pleased with myself for coming so far, hardly using my crutch at all. My depression lifted despite the buried weight within me. I sat quietly, abandoning myself to my senses.

In this way one may take in the feel of a country – by listening to it, its sounds distant and close by, minute and spatial, familiar and unidentifiable; by breathing it, and letting its intangibles make themselves known, as far as one is capable of apprehending them.

It was a sense of strength I took in from these hills and clearflowing burns, a heroic quality quite apart from their human history. Their sounds were like a sermon. How artificial, how perishable, New York seemed, and the vanities of southern California! The wild, cool, scented air reassured me, infused me with its vitality, gave me a calming all-over *answer* even if I couldn't quite decipher it.

I felt I understood Bart better here, his bigness of spirit which couldn't allow for pettiness, an attribute some people considered inflexible, or square. Lord Greggan's theory, quoted by Jean, that Scottish weather is character-building, may not be so far-fetched. Bart's strong-mindedness might have been a legacy from the land of his ancestors. I also felt

I understood Greggan of Strathburne better, who had never left this uncompromising wildness, had never been tamed by American affluence, had never learned to tolerate what he considered unworthy.

I brooded there for perhaps half an hour. I was deciding I'd better take up where I'd left off and head back to the castle, when a car approached from the direction of Kirkangus, and I recognized the silver-gray Lagonda and watched Jean and her father and Lady Fanquill pass by, their faces solemn with the look of people who have been to church. They must have recognized me as well. The car slowed, halted, and backed up.

Jean in the passenger's seat rolled down her window, which was nearest me. Lord Greggan was driving and Lady Fanquill, in a feathered hat that I believe is called a toque, sat in back.

"Are you all right, Mrs. MacLarkie?" called Jean.

"Oh, yes, perfectly!" I answered, with a great show of sprightliness. The last thing I wanted was to appear forlorn under their gaze, Greggan's in particular, and as if to bear out my words and prove I hadn't fallen by the wayside, I stood up. But I hadn't taken time to make sure of my balance and my legs were more tired than I realized, and I sat immediately down, hard.

My astonished face and subsequent idiot grin must have told the story.

Jean at once made to get out of the car but her father was ahead of her, crossing the road in three or four immense determined strides. He was more laird today than man-of-all-work, wearing a tidier kilt than usual, as well as shirt, tie, and "kilt jacket" with bone buttons on the braided cuffs and pocket flaps, and he was shaved and his flaxen hair neatly brushed; and this sprucing-up seemed to accentuate the deep blue of his eyes, or perhaps it was the look of pride-swallowing resolve that intensified them.

"You've walked a long way," he said, quite humanely. "Let us give you a ride home." He put a hand under my elbow to help me up. The set of his jaw indicated he would brook no argument; yet the deep blue eyes looked quickly and apprehensively into mine from under the blond brows as if part of him wouldn't blame me if I humiliated him by pulling away. He was obliged, come what may, to live up to his own standards of chivalry. I might be no less of a thorn to him than I'd been in the stable yard, but as Lady Fanquill had predicted, he could not as a nobleman permit ignoble behavior to go unrectified.

But I can't bear to see a proud man humble himself; my instinct is to rush in and spare him.

"Thank you," I said quickly, "that's very kind of you."

Once again the pupils of his eyes shrank in a wince. Gentleness evidently wounded him more than harshness. He set his jaw anew, his face became blank and remote as though to disguise his discomfort, and he guided me to the car.

Jean had hopped out and opened the rear door. Taking over from her father, she boosted me onto the old polished leather beside her aunt, and Greggan laid my crutch at my feet. Lady Fanquill welcome me as usual with a non sequitur: "It is not nearly as lugubrious as it looks, you know."

If she'd said *he* instead of *it*, I'd have understood her better.

Jean came to my rescue, asking, "What is not, Aunt Lydia?" as she resumed her seat beside her father. She is not daunted by her aunt's riddles.

"Why, Scotland, of course, my dear!"

"Of course, Aunt Lydia."

"But it doesn't look lugubrious to me," I said. "I looks ... august." It's a word I use as infrequently as lugubrious, but it pleased Lady Fanquill.

"How discriminating of you," she purred, gazing at me as if I'd outdone myself.

109

"And discreet," said Lord Greggan unexpectedly. He drove in a commanding way, knowing car and road so well he could travel at fairly high speed. Ordinarily I'd have been terrified, but my wits were occupied with conversation within the car, and I found I was again filled with rare exhilaration.

"I do not believe Mrs. MacLarkie finds it easy," rejoined his aunt, "to place discretion before candor. Is that not so, my dear? But perhaps you are prejudiced in Scotland's favor, being a landowner yourself."

We had come all at once alarmingly close to the source of the laird's resentment against me, or what I believed was the source, yet I had a curious notion Lady Fanquill was feeding me lines, or as they say in court, leading the witness. "I am only a lifetime owner," I reminded her.

"So you are," she said, gratified. I'd said the right thing. She, too, knew the terms of Bart's will. "However," she continued, veering off the delicate subject, "I detect a touch of the poet in you, if you will forgive so personal a remark. Poets always respond to the Highlands. Or, to put it another way, most Highlanders have a way with words. For example, it is not so much what the Reverend Thornhill says that mesmerizes one, as how he says it."

Jean sent a sardonic glance over her shoulder. "Like father, like son."

"No," said Lady Fanquill. "The son does not preach."

"I should think not," said Jean with a smile.

I inquired about the church in Kirkangus, whether it was very old and so on, and Jean told me it was only eighteenth century, and asked if I'd seen the castle's medieval chapel. I said I hadn't, and at that point we arrived at the causeway, and the buff-colored walls loomed before us. Involuntarily I took in a breath, to be let out as a sigh, but stopped myself in time and swallowed it.

Nevertheless Jean must have heard me. She said, "You'll be glad to have your brother-in-law with you, won't you? I sometimes think our women guests have a dull time of it. Does he shoot?"

Does Colin shoot? Knowing Colin, I nearly laughed. "I'm not sure," I answered. Hadn't Bart said something about hunting in the Rockies when they were boys? "But Colin never needs to be amused. He's amusing in his own right. And neither are we women having a dull time. We do as we please and go our separate ways, and thank goodness, I can stand on my own two feet now."

"Aye," spoke up Lord Greggan again, "so we

noticed this morning." I broke into laughter, and I observed an uncommon indentation in Greggan's cheek, like the dimple of a smile; I wished I could see his whole face. A smile undoubtedly produced an interesting transformation.

Jean laughed, too, and as we drew up in the courtyard she said, "Come and have tea with us this afternoon, and we'll show you the chapel afterward."

I accepted the invitation, and then, before Munro could reach us, Greggan was out of the car and opening the rear door. He helped Lady Fanquill out, and after her, myself.

Face to face with him, his unreadable stare confronting me, his hand circling my wrist, I felt once more the weakening sweep of attraction to him, my knees, thighs, and breasts caught up consecutively in a vertical vibration of purest desire.

It must, it must be a displaced longing for Bart! A Scot, Greggan must be a symbol for Bart! (In the middle of the night I cry out at myself with written words.) How else explain this irrelevant passion for a broody, cross-grained man, barely an acquaintance, and Bart not a year dead! How otherwise excuse this madness: poised there in the courtyard, with Jean and Lady Fanquill and Munro looking on,

I might easily, given the slightest encouragement, have melted into Greggan's arms.

It was over in a second, he let go of my wrist (had he felt the tremble in it?), and I turned and went up the steps, trying to catch my breath as if I'd been running.

"What a mistake," mused Lady Fanquill apropos of heaven knows what, as we passed through the double doors, "to believe that life holds no more delights, and no more dangers."

II. . . .

Dottie returned from Inverness in time for lunch, and we were all on our best behavior, as we've tried to be since our blowup on the road from Kirkangus. The atmosphere was greatly relaxed, and I could almost believe the buildup of strain between us existed only in my own mind.

As we paused afterward in the upstairs hall Lilah said if I'd no objections she'd take the car and go exploring. "I don't suppose you'd care to go with me, Sue?"

I hope my face didn't show my inner recoil. "No, thank you!" I added more calmly, "I'm having tea with Jean and her father and they're going to show me the castle chapel."

"Oh?" she said with that slight inquisitiveness which puts my back up, and today set my teeth on edge. "Well, that's nice, dear," and she turned politely to Dottie.

"Count me out, too," said Dottie quickly. "After my snooze I gotta get my Sunday letter off to Sam."

Lilah made a wide bright smile. "Each to his own, then!"

And suddenly contrite, as I so often am with Lilah, guessing there may have been hurt feelings behind that smile, I wished her a happy afternoon, said, "Till dinner then!" and blew her a kiss as we scattered to our rooms.

There was much that might have kept me awake when I lay down on my bed, in particular my intermittent lust for the Earl of Strathburne, but I went off at once into an obliterating sleep.

I woke up at four o'clock thinking, knowing, *She was there.* In my sleep I'd heard Bart's voice saying, "Don't hurry, Lilah, we're not going out until six." Did she come for lunch? How did we spend the afternoon? Were we together at all times, never separated? At least, never separated for the time it takes to tamper with the brakes of a car?

I could remember nothing more. The cloud closed again over the terrible day. But I had the answer to Dottie's first unsettling question.

114

Lilah was there, at the house, the day of the accident.

"Are you going into the hotel business, too, Severn, like your cousin Gordon?" Severn was conducting me to the private quarters where Jean and her father lived. By now I knew he was another relative.

"No, mistress. I'm going to be a keeper."

We had traversed the courtyard and were passing under an arch into a stone tunnel, making our way to an outer court, or ward. A sharp wind had risen to bluster about the castle walls and spit a few drops of rain, and I was glad I'd worn the mohair stole that goes with my rose-colored wool suit.

"A keeper, Severn? Like Dougal, you mean?"

"Aye, a gamekeeper. I'll study forestry as well. The laird is sending me to school."

"Ah, lucky Severn. Most of your life you'll be out of doors."

He gave me a quick smile, the upper blushes registering. "You understand," he said softly.

"If I were a man I'd want that, too." We emerged from the tunnel into the smaller court, and headed for still another passageway. "Will you be keeper and forester for the laird?"

"Aye, when Dougal retires." He added proudly, "They take me along already for the hind cull."

"The hind cull?" It had a disagreeable sound.

"Every year," he explained as if by rote, "the Deer Commission requires the lairds to cull a number of hinds out of the herds on their estates."

"Then by culling you mean — shooting?"

"Aye. The stalking begins in a few days."

I didn't like the sound of *stalking* either. Everything, since I woke from my nap, seemed to strike a sinister note. "Does the laird take part in the stalking?"

"Oh certainly, mistress. It's for the good of the herds. The laird is the best marksman in the Highlands. He never misses. A good stalker only shoots to kill. If ever he misses and wounds a creature, he tracks the beast down no matter how far it takes him, to put it out of its agony."

My shoulders hunched and I drew my stole more tightly around me. It wasn't hard to picture those piercing eyes sighting down the barrel of a rifle.

We had come to one of the immense drum towers that punctuate the outer walls, and we halted before a deep-set door, unlocked like almost all the castle doors. Severn pressed an old-fashioned china button set in brass, and turned to me. "I enjoy our wee chats, mistress.

I regret it when they end."

"So do I, Severn." Footsteps descending on stone sounded within.

His face glowed with all four blushes. "Good evening, then!" And he left me.

Jean appeared in the vestibule to greet me. "I hope you can manage these curving steps, Mrs. MacLarkie. There's barely room for two abreast, but I'll lend a hand from above if you like." She led the way.

I'm better at going up than down and I took the steps without help. I said, "Since I call you Jean as everyone else does, will you call me Susan?"

"Yes," she replied simply, glancing back, "I'd like to."

I was prepared for living quarters to go with the glowering drum tower (with the glowering Earl of Strathburne, for that matter), draped with dark tapestries and festooned with weapons, but we came out in an eighteenth-century apartment of chintzes, flowers, and mellowed woods. Off the hall a hearth fire burned in a small drawing room, elegant and inviting.

"My father will be along soon," Jean told me as we settled ourselves on a sofa before a Georgian tea service. "He usually makes a walking tour of the estate on Sunday."

I was struggling with a huge mental readjustment. It was easy enough to picture Greggan stalking the hills with a gun, but if these were his possessions, even if inherited from better days, his early prints of birds, his glowing eighteenth-century horse paintings, his finely bound volumes on flora and fauna, then he was far more civilized than I'd assumed. This was the habitat of a scholar, a naturalist with a taste for beauty. Perhaps the cherished Lagonda should have given me a clue.

I couldn't let the opportunity pass to learn more about this contradictory man. "Managing such a place," I answered Jean, seizing the first opening that came to mind, "must keep him busy from dawn to dusk."

"Aye, he puts his hand to everything." She was quite unreserved. "He's often mistaken for the most lowly employee on the place."

"A mistake I made myself."

"Don't let it embarrass you." She handed me my cup of tea. "He plays the part to the hilt."

"He enjoys it?"

"Why, it's protective coloring! It serves a double purpose. It keeps people at a distance, and it conceals the fact that he is an anachronism. Why devote oneself to holding such an obsolete domain together?" Her cynicism was a pretense, I knew; her eyes twinkled. "What can it possibly mean to anyone, in this day and age?

Family ties, the love of place — all went out with the horse and carriage, wouldn't you say?"

"I would say it's what lacking in this day and age," I told her. "I would say it's what's called a sense of responsibility."

"And how out of date *that* is!" But she was pleased with me, and she dropped her flippant tone. "Och, there are no limits to his devotion. He feels responsible not only for his own people but for the people and the land of the region. He takes part in local politics and promotes the reforestation programs. A relic of feudalism he may be, but he's hard-working, and there's not a phony ounce in him."

"Yet he keeps people at a distance," I murmured, still prompting.

"Ah, well, you see," she gazed at the tea tray as if wavering now between reserve and unreserve, "men do that, don't they, when they've pinned their faith on someone and — and been unlucky."

I felt a pang then. There was a note of despair in Jean's voice, and I sensed the extent of her father's hurt, and hers.

"To be sure, he doesn't give an impression of softness," she went on, replacing the lid of the teapot with a little silvery plop as if this were her final word on the subject, "but he is, in fact, a tender-hearted man."

So Lady Fanquill had said, too. I couldn't lose the picture of the steady eye behind the gunsight, shooting to kill, but I respected both women and I wanted to believe them. There was no question that a number of people, related and unrelated, owed their livelihood and their well-being to the earl; there was no question that he had saved my life.

"Well, Jean," I said, "I'd take your word for anything."

She answered at once, "And I yours."

We exchanged a smile of cemented friendship.

I asked, "Lady Fanquill isn't coming to tea?"

"She thought it would be a good idea for us to get to know each other. I thought so too. Have some almond cake. I made it myself."

We ate cake and sipped tea and watched the brightly burning fire. "Jock, too, plays a part to the hilt, doesn't he?"

"Ha," she scoffed, but good-naturedly. "If he does, he's obvious as a child."

"That's what I mean. He wants one to believe he's frivolous and on the make, while underneath he's actually quite serious and perceptive."

She put down her teacup, her eyes widening. "Gordon — serious?"

I met her stare. "I think so."

She had explained her father to me, to make me view him in a more favorable light; I was doing the same for her with Gordon. It was she who'd told me, Don't be fooled by the barriers men build.

She made a little face. "Okay, Susan, I shall have to live up to my promise and take your word for it. At least, I'll keep it in mind. But maybe you see Gordon as serious because you're serious yourself."

"And perceptive!"

She leaned back and gave up the argument with a bubble of laughter.

The fire popped comfortably. I said, "You know I have property here, Jean?" She said she did. It was a silly question; everyone knew. "You don't hold it against me?"

She faced me. "I hold nothing against you." She was so emphatic that I wondered if she were declaring herself a partisan, taking a stand opposed to her father's. I'd always felt she was prejudiced in my favor.

"I went to see a solicitor about the land yesterday," I told her, "the spryest, shiniest, foxiest solicitor I've ever met —"

"Archibald MacBaine!"

We laughed. "Aye, Archibald. He's going to send me a map; and then, would you be good enough to find someone to drive me there, wherever the land is, and let me see it?" I added, since we were friends, "My husband meant to come."

She studied me. "I'll attend to it," she told me softly.

At that moment we heard heavy leather soles on the stone steps, and a few seconds later Greggan of Strathburne strode in, followed by a huge man in gray with a dog-collar who could only be the Reverend Thornhill.

III. . . .

"Had to trundle Gordon out," boomed the minister, plunging across the room to Jean. "Red hornet ailing, carburetor or some such. What a comedown, to have to beg a ride in his dad's great Rover. But he was amiable withal." He kissed Jean's brow. "Ran across your father, who invited me in. The sight of you makes up for missing my soccer match on the telly." He glared at me. "And this must be Mrs. MacLurkie from California, word of whose beauty has traveled o'er banks and braes." He shook my hand vigorously. "Aye, a heroine from Sir Walter Scott, thou art." He had the build of a prizefighter and the voice of an opera singer. His hair, which might once have been auburn like Gordon's, was gray but thick and curling. "Well, then, a cup o' tea for me, my bonnie

Jean, and I'll be off again." He carried his cup to a chair and crouched over it, sipping thirstily, tucking in a slice of almond cake as well, his fingers nimble and quite dainty, and thundered away on the subject of soccer.

I knew now where Gordon got his energy, and I could imagine the Reverend Thornhill in the pulpit, spellbinding his congregation with a mellifluous variety of vocal registers.

I turned to Jean to find she had pink cheeks like a flattered girl of twelve. Well, I reasoned, if she adores Gordon's father, she ought to adore Gordon.

In the turbulence created by the clergyman I'd almost lost track of Lord Greggan. He had gone to stand with his back to the fire, an amused light in his eyes, and for the first time I saw him at rest, not fishing, not washing a car, not driving. He made an interesting contrast to his friend. Where the Reverend Thornhill seemed straining to burst his physical bounds, Greggan was at home within himself, yet in his quietness all the more impressive. He isn't tall by American standards, just under six feet, but he brought indoors with him some of the heroic quality of the hills.

With his Sunday kilt he wore a handsome badger-head sporran bound in silver, and a dagger, the traditional *sgian dubh*, set with cairngorms, in his stocking, and one beheld him now as seigneur, chief of the clan, protector of the family, preserver of the domain, and upholder of the faith — all the factors which add up in theory to an anachronism; only there was nothing theoretical about him, standing, feet apart, before his hearth. His coloring alone gave him brilliance. He was a valid man, combining, hawklike, both wildness and natural discipline, a living force independent of time and moral fashion.

His eyes, meeting mine, moved away. I was the enemy in his camp. And his physical impact on me, my mixed responses, my disadvantage in his home, discomfited me, and I debated how soon I could leave.

"Was everything in order on your walk, Dad?" asked Jean, drawing him into the conversation. She held out his cup.

"Aye, but the sky's lowering." He moved to accept his cup and returned to the fire. "The wind's got up from the north."

"Snow on the peaks tonight!" said Thornhill.

"I saw Mrs. Andrew MacLarkie at the far end of the loch," Gregan continued. He didn't look in my direction but I realized he was addressing me. "She was parked over Craggy Head. She must have found the dirt road. There's a fine view from Craggy Head, but a dangerous drop.

124

She's a good driver, I hope?"

"None better," I answered. "She doesn't look the type, but there isn't much she doesn't know about cars."

The Reverend Thornhill chose that moment, thank God, to create a titanic diversion by rising and taking his leave. "Speaking of cars," he cried, "I must climb into mine and away to evensong!" He bent over Jean again, bowed to me, saluted Greggan, and bounded from the room.

But I had heard Bart's voice again, his last cry, "The brakes, Susan –!" and felt the blood drain from my face downward to explode about my lungs. Lilah had driven for years for the Red Cross, she had taken a course in mechanics, there wasn't much she didn't know about cars . . .

I swallowed, the blood returned to my face, the room righted itself. Greggan, having seen the minister out, was returning from the hall.

"I must go, too," I said. "May I see the chapel on my way back?"

"Certainly," said Jean, turning to me, still smiling after the ungainly Thornhill. I wonder about Jean: did she make up her mind in that second or had she planned this all along? Is she trying to break down her father's MacLarkie-prejudice? She got to her feet, saying, "I should go over and relieve Miss Pinwherry. She likes an early supper and she's been on the job all day. Dad will show you — won't you, Dad?"

Poor Dad! He could neither rudely refuse nor eagerly assent. "Of course," he said, a hint of irony touching his lips, produced in all likelihood by the lengths to which chivalry was driving him. Jean was putting him to the test.

I rose also, unable to back out of the situation without making it even more awkward. Jean and I said our good-byes warmly, and then Greggan was leading me without further delay through the hall to a door in the paneling. "We'll take the shortest way," he said.

We filed through a passage in the thick wall of the tower itself, and stepped straight out onto an open walk atop the castle wall. The stormy sky hung close over us, its dark clouds hurrying. The walk was about six feet wide and protected by low parapets, but even so the loch far below seemed to shift under my eyes. I needed to hold onto something.

"Give me a minute!" I cried into the wind, and Greggan glanced back. "I'm not very good at heights!"

"Look down at your feet!" But he could see that wasn't much help. Perhaps I actually swayed. He came toward me.

I had a terrible thought then, I don't know

why, except that I have built up so much inner alarm, and so much mistrust; I've begun to shy like a terror-haunted horse. The close black boiling sky and the north wind added to my fright. I must have been quite disoriented. I thought: *He could kill me now.*

He could reverse his heedless rescue from the loch and force me over the parapet, back into the dark water, he could say I'd lost my balance while his back was turned, and my land would be his and his MacLarkie-hatred avenged.

It was the perfect opportunity. In the few moments before we left his drawing room he might even have planned it.

IV. . . .

I must have shrunk back toward the door. I let out a little strangled mew as he reached me, and put up my hands.

He said quite softly, "There now." He took my flapping stole and wound it around me, high around my neck so that my face was half-buried. Then he stepped beside me and put a strong arm around my shoulders.

"Come," he said in my ear. "Put your head down and let me guide you."

It was useless to resist. I tried to make myself have faith in him. But as I put one foot out, and then another, I didn't know if I were going to my death or not. I moved like a robot.

And then we came to another drum tower. He opened the door and we stepped inside. I stood trembling for a moment.

"All right, are you?"

"Yes," I gasped doubtfully. I was almost more afraid of myself then, and my insane imaginings, than of him. I tried to collect myself, and I peered down the curving stone steps.

"I was only trying to spare you a lot of unnecessary walking," he said. "The ground-level way is very roundabout. Give me your crutch and take my hand."

We descended painstakingly, one step at a time, and now I was too preoccupied with saving my neck from a fall to imagine things anymore, and I was certainly beyond indulging in wanton vibrations over the touch of his hand. We reached the bottom, he returned my crutch, and I stood for a second or two catching my breath and letting the blood settle in brain and heart.

"You seem to be forever coming to my rescue," I breathed. "I haven't convalesced, I guess, as much as I like to think."

"It's hardly fair to test yourself in Scotland," he said, and there was again a glimmer of humor in his expression. In the damp, dimly lit chamber we spoke in murmurs, almost intimately. My panic may have made him forget, at least for the moment, his enmity. "It's a very uneven country."

"It's a very uneven castle," I answered.

"It is so," he agreed. "You might do better with a cane."

He took a breath then, squaring his shoulders, perhaps rearming himself with antagonism, and we went out into a narrow alley where the walls crowded close about a deep-set door, so nearly hidden that I wondered if it had been deliberately disguised in times of religious strife. Beckoning me to follow, Greggan opened the door.

We were in the chapel. It was almost totally dark, but the churchly odor was unmistakable.

"Wait here while I light the candles."

I waited.

The altar, the vaulted nave, came glimmeringly to life. My mouth fell open.

It is a jewel, his chapel. About forty feet long, the stone is the same tawny stuff that the castle is made of, but here the walls, arches, and ceiling were whitewashed and then tenderly decorated in red and blue and gold, the designs interwoven with flowers and leaves, lambs and fishes, and all manner of symbols, the ribs of the arches joined with bosses of gilded thistles.

My indrawn breath ended in a wonder-struck gasp.

"Aye, it's charming, isn't it?" Greggan had returned from the altar. "The Reformists no doubt would have called it papist, but thank God it was spared, for the door was sealed off, and its lack of ventilation preserved it almost intact. It has a welcome, hasn't it? We'll sit a moment, shall we?"

He chose one of the rearmost benches where we could look down the aisle to the radiant altar. If I hadn't seen his drawing room or himself at home in it, I'd have thought he hadn't the aesthetic grace to use the word *charming* or to make an apt metaphor. *Welcome* was exactly what the chapel had. Even in the stable yard I'd noted his ability to switch from Scots vernacular to King's English, and again I had to acknowledge a person of taste and intellect behind the facade of brawn and valor. Protective coloring, Jean had called it.

It was strange indeed to sit in cloistered silence beside this man whose complexity kept jarring me off base. I wished hopelessly that it were possible to shake hands with him, make peace, and start over.

I closed my eyes. Something very unholy must have been building up in me all day, or wearing me down. The instant I closed my eyes nightmarish fears leapt out of hiding. I almost cried out. A sense of danger rushed upon me and crowded me on all sides, even there in the chapel, so that even my breath became labored.

Please! I begged of the silence, the hush of ageless reverence. If the single word were a prayer, it was more fatalistic than faithful. I was lost in a labyrinth of my own doubts, and alone, as alone as in the bottomless loch.

"Convalesced from what?" asked Greggan.

I started. He still sat with his arms folded, his eyes gazing at the altar. For a moment I couldn't think what he meant. "Oh." He was referring to my disadvantage in uneven Scotland. "From an accident. An automobile accident."

"Too bad," he said, dismissingly I thought in my unhappy state, if not self-righteously, as if automobile accidents were a consequence of living in the remote, impure world beyond the Highlands.

It was like a slap in the face, I felt, coming on top of my desperation.

"Yes," I answered, "it *was* too bad." Did he think he was the only one who had tasted bitterness? "My husband was killed and I lost my baby. I nearly died, too."

His arms came slowly unfolded and he turned to me. I couldn't tell if his eyes were grieved or angry; just then I didn't care. I'd had enough of protective barriers, his and mine.

"But in some ways pain and loss have had a good effect on me," I went on, and I listened, amazed, to the words tumbling out in a low hoarse voice. "I'm no less cowardly, or less easily confused, or less foolishly hurt, but at the same time I'm less indifferent to the pain of others, and I have less inclination to keep people at a distance, and less need to be always right." I had to finish quickly before tears cut me off. "I know you had no choice but to bring me here, Lord Greggan, but thank you anyway."

I got to my feet and moved into the aisle.

He caught up with me at the door. He turned me about, his hand on my upper arm. There was grief and anger in both our eyes, and this time I did melt. His arms encircled me and grasped me to himself, he bore down in a bruising kiss, opening my lips to his mouth, his powerful thighs spread convulsively against mine. I don't think he meant to do this at all. I think both of us were acting out longing and despair, expressing rage at life with life's own volcanic force, meeting separate bitterness with a kind of bitter oneness.

But we were too encumbered with sporrans and stoles and tweeds and buckles to progress beyond his straining embrace, and we broke apart when our lungs, our pounding blood, our focalized loins, were close to bursting.

"There, now, Mrs. MacLarkie!"

I took a step backward. "My name is Susan!"

"Aye, for Jean. Well, come, then. Did y'ever make love in a chapel before?"

We stared at each other, both of us, I swear, disbelieving. And yet I knew if he wanted me here, now, I would satisfy even his need for revenge.

But the door burst open as we stared, and I was thankful we had stepped apart.

My brother-in-law, Colin MacLarkie, stood there.

CHAPTER 7

I. . . .

"I couldn't wait another day to see you, love!"
We were strolling back through the lamplit
alleys and courtyards to the castle's main entrance, I slightly punch-drunk, he babbling
companionably, his arm tucked under mine.
Colin all over: he has to establish a cozy,
affectionate rapport with people and he can't
help saying first what will please most.

Then, second, he passed lightly on to the
truth. "I was planning to come tomorrow and
wire ahead and do it all properly, but my chums
went off this morning to visit their mums and I
couldn't face one of those empty London Sun-
days, so I up and got on a plane and rented a car
and made tracks for Castle Strathburne, trusting the prestige of my sister-in-law to get me a
room, which of course it did, and the blushing
boy told me where to look for you. Darling, that
was the laird you just introduced me to, wasn't
it? It couldn't have been anyone else,

in that marvelous getup!"

"It was himself." Another nice thing about Colin is if you aren't feeling talkative yourself, he is perfectly willing to carry the ball, chatting away and filling in the gaps, and on the other hand, when you do have something to say he listens intently. I was trying now to control the tremble which had set in, up and down my body, in reaction to the contretemps with Greggan, a clash far more devastating than the one in the stable yard. My eyelids and upper lip had broken out in perspiration, and I touched a Kleenex to my face, knowing Colin misses very little with his bright dark MacLarkie eyes.

"He's like a Wyeth illustration," he went on, "in one of those novels Bart used to read when we were kids. Or are you too young to know what I'm talking about?"

"I know what you're talking about. Bart kept his best-loved childhood books. N. C. Wyeth, you mean, the father of Andrew. Yes, Greggan is very much like."

"The flaxen hair, the far-sighted blue eyes, the muscles. All he needs is a shield and a white tabard over a coat of mail."

"And a claymore, too."

"By all means, a claymore! I don't know what it means but it sounds deadly. He's not overly friendly, is he? If I were thin-skinned I'd say he disliked me on sight." The fact is, Colin *is* thin-skinned; at least, he's subtly receptive to another's thoughts and feelings. "I didn't interrupt something, did I? I thought the atmosphere seemed a bit – *charged*. Sue, you're walking so beautifully! You've hardly any limp at all!"

He also has an artful way of changing an uncomfortable subject, or dropping it, for the time being, before you have a chance to prevaricate. But I knew it wasn't the last I'd hear from him about the laird. We had come into the stronger light of the entrance and he turned to study me at arm's length.

I could see Colin better, too, in this light, and my breath caught in my throat, he looked so much like Bart. The curling dark hair, the black brows, the white skin that doesn't suntan; their Celtic heritage. But Colin's features are more finely drawn than Bart's, the bones of the nose chiseled, the curve of the lips firmer; Bart's nose was broken in college athletics, and he was a bigger man in every way. Colin was the artistic one.

"Oh, Sue-love," he murmured, shaking his head, "you're more breathtaking than ever. No, don't shrink, it's time you got over that complex. You've filled out a little. You're positively *vivid*. Is it that fearsome nurse of yours who's worked such a miracle? Or dear devoted Lilah? Or could it be the manly laird?" He chuckled, stepped back to my side, and gave my shoulders a one-armed hug. "Whoever is working it, it delights my soul. I've always wanted to see you like this."

We proceeded up the steps into the hall. I told him I had a little business to attend to and would join him for dinner later.

"A little business?" He cocked his head. "How you've changed! You're managing your own affairs at last, are you? I knew you could, given half a chance. All right, we'll meet in the bar in half an hour — with Lilah and your nurse, of course. We must all be chums." I hadn't so much as glanced at his tight-fitting denims and gold chains but in his mind-reading way he added, "Don't worry, I'll change. I picked up some gorgeous gear in London, you won't know me from Michael Caine. Ta, love, until later." With a butterfly kiss on the eyebrow (covertly observed by Severn and Munro), he left me.

The instant he'd gone I went and shut myself into the glass and mahogany telephone booth at the end of the hall. A delayed reaction commenced. I felt stunned, not so much by Greggan's abandon as by my total response to it. How long had this tempestuous potential lain dormant in me? But for Colin's sudden appearance, Greggan and I might at this moment be picking ourselves up from the stone floor. It was unthinkable, so far removed from sanity, let alone decency, that I felt the bubbling of hysterical laughter.

I quieted down, thankful no one could see me, thankful Jean was in a huddle with Miss Pinwherry — thankful, too, that Colin had arrived with his facade of frivolity, his balloon-pricking cunning, his easy camaraderie. From now on, I wouldn't be so much at my own mercy.

As I'd hoped, a local directory hung from a chain. I flipped through the pages to the *M*s.

Yes, there were two listings. Mrs. Kenzie MacLarkie, The Rowans, Kirkangus 27. Murdo MacLarkie, Kirkangus 521.

I copied the names in my little purse notebook, left the booth, and went upstairs.

II. . . .

I was stripping off my tweed suit when there was a hesitant knock on the hall door. "Come in, dear!" No one but Lilah knocks in that way.

She was quite pretty in a white lace blouse and long lavender wool skirt. "Did you have a nice time?" She shut the door behind her. "Did you see the chapel?"

I studied her, trying to see beyond the pale innocent eyes, rather myopic, beyond the old-fashioned-valentine effect of her costume. Since being with Greggan I had actually forgotten: *She was at the house the day of the accident* . . .

"Oh, Sue, what is it? Why are you looking at me like that?"

"Sorry, darling, I was miles away." I moved to my dressing table to redo my makeup.

"Are you still upset about yesterday? Coming home from Kirkangus?"

I could hardly remember yesterday. "No," I told her truthfully. "Not any more."

"You *know* it wasn't my fault, don't you? You *remember* my telling you the handbrake was hard to pull on?"

"Yes, I do, Lilah."

"But I was *sure* I had it on all the way, before I left the car. I can't understand it. Dottie didn't touch it, did she, after I left?"

My arms, uplifted, froze. "Why would Dottie touch it?"

"Only if . . ." She halted. She glanced at the connecting door and dropped her voice. "Only if she *wanted* the car to roll a little, and then she could catch it, and make you rely on her that much more and rely on me that much less!"

"Oh my God, Lilah." *Two* paranoiacs!

"When I left the car you had your eyes shut,

139

you were upset about the fog. She could have done it when you —" The look on my face must have stopped her.

"Lilah," I said softly, "you have a right to think whatever you want to think. But I choose to believe what happened yesterday was an —" I couldn't make myself utter the word *accident* anymore "— was bad luck. Probably we wouldn't have rolled very far, there were trees or bushes behind us. Anyway, I ask you not to bring it up again. I've had enough of personality conflicts." I turned to finish my makeup. "And by the way, Colin has arrived."

"Well! Did you know he was coming today?"

"No, but he has never gone in for announcing his arrival ahead of time. Lilah, I won't have another conflict between you and Colin."

She was silent a moment and then she said calmly, "I know. I don't want any more of it either. I could have tried harder and I *will* try harder, with Colin *and* Dottie. I don't care for Colin, you know that, but I'll do my best to look on the good side of him. He *is* amusing, and you deserve to laugh and enjoy your trip."

Disarmed again, I might have felt the old contrition and tried to make it up to her. Did she always count on that? But Colin was right, I was changing. And in a curious way the scene in the chapel had stiffened my backbone. I said,

"Thank you," firmly. I stood up, went to the wardrobe, and took out a simple dark dress.

Lilah faced me. She looked pitiful now, clasping her little bag to her breast, her eyes swimming. "Susan, Susan," she cried in a low voice, "have patience with me! All my life I've had to have patience with myself!"

So I went to her after all and put my arms around her. "Have patience with me, too, Lilah. I'm not my mild-dispositioned self any more. The earth has been shaken under me." I gave her a final hug and broke away. "Will you zip me up, please? Come on, it's time to go down." I knocked on the connecting door. "Ready, Dottie?"

"Ready!" she called, and Lilah and I left my room to meet her in the hall.

III. . . .

We were quite the merriest guests in the hotel tonight.

Colin, most presentable in navy-blue blazer and gray flannels, cheered us up from the moment we joined him in the bar. He kissed Lilah as though there had never been anything but fondness between them, and from then on lavished a puppyish warmth on her that wouldn't accept anything but warmth in return. He teased her, and he knew just how far to go,

141

only carrying his teasing to the point of making her smile in spite of herself.

With Dottie O. he felt his way, being at first drolly respectful, then exaggeratedly gallant. But in the dining room he tucked his napkin neatly over his lap, leaned toward her in a confiding way, and said, "There've been a lot of stories about sadistic nurses. Are you a sadistic nurse?"

"Hafta be," Dottie replied calmly. "Ask Susan. What else d'you wanta know?"

"Do you have a sex life?"

Lilah's jaw dropped.

Dottie looked at him levelly. "Any chance I get."

After that they were off, like two ribald old burlesque artists trying to top each other. The other guests must have thought we'd all had too much to drink. Mrs. Barsington-Banks glared at us over her husband's head. I was grateful for the laughter and joined in it. It kept my mind from private turmoil.

Jock's formal, attentive, dining room mask was more inscrutable than ever; perhaps he didn't know how to take the drastic change at his table of quiet ladies. Colin, watching him sprint about, called him Scotland's answer to automation.

At the end of the meal Colin raised his glass.

142

"To you, Lilah and Dottie, for transforming my sister-in-law from ghost to goddess!" What did he mean by *ghost*? There's always a little catch in Colin's flattery, a hint of acid truth, which prevents one's feeling entirely flattered. They drank. "So," he said, "that launches my campaign. I'm going to make Susan stop hiding her light under a bushel if it's the last thing I do!" I tried to laugh.

Afterward in the lounge I introduced Colin to Lady Fanquill.

Her vague eyes came to rest on him. She looked very regal. "What is your magic?" she demanded. "The castle has quite come to life!"

Colin made a low bow. "But that is my lot, madam. I am but a poor wandering minstrel, livening the weary hours for my betters in exchange for a crust of bread and a cup of wine."

Lady Fanquill uttered a tinkling laugh and went along with his charade. "Well-spoken, rogue. But take care. Minstrels sometimes know too much for their own good."

"Oh, I do know far too much, my lady, and I am very careful. A good minstrel sees all, tells nothing."

I gave him a quick glance; so did Lilah and Dottie. There were after all a number of people who might feel uneasy at a remark like that.

Lady Fanquill tapped him on the shoulder. "A good minstrel is sometimes not what he seems. Sometimes he is an exiled knight in disguise. Sometimes he is a spy, sent to undermine the castle." She made a little triangular smile, rather flirtatious. "Be warned. We at Strathburne are wise in the ways of the naughty world."

Colin turned to us. "She has found me out. I am undone." We joined again in laughter.

I've stayed awake long enough to put it all down.

Bart, what's happening to me?

But it's no use. My pleas fall short of Bart's threshold. His distance is too far and today is too near. I'm no longer sure he hears or sees me. To the living there seems almost a smugness in the silence of the dead; nothing can reach them, nothing disturb them. I make a disturbance, calling out, but the answering silence is like a stony indifference.

I look back on our marriage and for the first time view it dimly, as if I'd been somewhat dim myself. *Did* I hide my life under a bushel? Freudian slip! Light, not life. But no one, not even Bart, ever called me vivid before.

Am I taking Colin's flattery too seriously after all?

And what do the deep blue eyes of Greggan, Earl of Strathburne, see, when they look at me? Do they see only a MacLarkie? Do they see his downfall, Woman?

Horrible; that moment high on the castle wall when he came toward me in the half-dark and I wondered if he meant to force me over the edge! And later, in the chapel, when I felt danger closing on me.

I must sleep. I can't go on in such fear, shrinking from one person and then another. I am building a ghastly tangle of suspicion about myself, suspicion that may be entirely unwarranted. If I go on like this I could lose my reason.

There is only one thing to do. Since I cannot protect myself from an unknown adversary in any case, I will abandon the effort. I make a resolve: I will harbor no more suspicions of anyone.

CHAPTER 8

I. . . .

"Mrs. MacLarkie? Mrs. Kenzie MacLarkie?"

Armed with pence and instructions from Severn, I was back in the phone booth this morning. It was a little before nine; none of my party had come downstairs yet. I liked the sound of Kenzie, a bit like cozy, better than Murdo, a bit like murder. "The Rowans" suggested a suburban house, whereas Murdo's number with its three digits rather than two might mean he lived in an outlying district — in the hills or on a lonely moor.

"Yes?" The voice was elderly but brisk, a no-nonsense voice.

I was all prepared with a bright telephone manner. "This is Mrs. Barton MacLarkie, from California. I'm staying at Castle Strathburne for a few weeks, and I thought I'd look up my husband's — my late husband's — relatives, if any. Would it be convenient if I came to call on you sometime soon?"

146

And to my amazement Mrs. Kenzie sucked in her breath in a shrill gasp. "You're a Mrs. MacLarkie, staying at *Strathburne?*"

"That's right. Mrs. Barton MacLarkie —"

There was a pause at Mrs. Kenzie's end. She seemed thunderstruck. Then she seemed to consider, and then to make up her mind. She said at last, "Aye, ye may come. Come the day, if ye like. The house is at the end of town, anyone can direct ye."

"Would this morning —"

"Aye, aye, this morning, whenever ye say." She squeezed da-ay and sa-ay high on the palate. She sounded neither eager nor put upon, but simply short. Mrs. Kenzie Mac-Larkie didn't waste her own or anyone else's time. She hung up.

I hurried back to my room and knocked on the connecting door. "Dottie, are you awake?" I was half-whispering.

"Am I awake: are you kidding? Come in." She was in a white tailored slip and about to don a navy skirt and orange wool pullover.

"Dottie, will you drive me to Kirkangus?"

"Sure, sure. Where's the fire?"

"I'm going to call on a local Mrs. MacLarkie, but I'd just as soon not have to explain it all to Lilah and Colin. If we leave before they're up — I mean —"

"Say no more, kiddo." She finished dressing. "We can take the back stairs that go down to the drive."

"And on the way home will you give me a driving lesson?"

She threw on a green raincoat and grabbed a red purse. "You don't need a driving lesson. All you need is muscle to put on the brakes. And gumption. Seems to me you're developing both. Let's go."

There was snow on the peaks, as Mr. Thornhill had predicted. Against the distant sky they looked sugar-dusted. It was a still cold morning with thin sunlight. The gold and bronze of autumn foliage seemed to have sprung out overnight along the loch-road. It was a peaceful landscape, but its stillness had a withdrawn appearance, a look of secrecy, or of waiting. Not a living creature stirred.

We talked about Colin on the drive to Kirkangus. Dottie's attitude toward him is amused and tolerant and a little skeptical, which is almost everyone's attitude; it was Bart's. It is one Colin himself cultivates. Dottie agreed his arrival had radically improved the atmosphere. We stayed off the subject of Lilah entirely and I was glad of that. I didn't want to tell Dottie what I remembered about the day of

148

the accident in California. I was determined today to believe it didn't mean anything, and I wasn't going to give Dottie the opportunity to make me think it did.

The Rowans is near the end of the street of neat gray houses, perhaps a little more spacious than the rest with its lawn and its two ornamental trees with orange berries (mountain ash in the States) — the house of a moderately prosperous small-town merchant.

Dottie left me off at the front gate. "I want to shop for some wool," she told me. "I think I'll start an afghan. I should be parked here when you come out."

Just imagining an afghan created by Dottie made my eyes blink.

I went up the walk and rang the bell and a tiny woman with tiny round clear eyes opened the door. She wore a clean blue Mother Hubbard with short sleeves over a blue sweater with long sleeves, and her hair was a mixture of ginger and blond with a few strands of white. It was plastered to her head in a small tight waves, and at the back, I discovered when she turned, it merged into small tight braids which chased each other around a sort of plaque at the nape of her neck. It was such a neat and intricate production that I wondered how she found time each morning to arrange it, for I judged from her work-dress and her shiny oaken hall that she devoted the forenoon to keeping a spotless house. On second thought I realized it must be a hairstyle dating back to her girlhood and decided from her quick movements that she undoubtedly wove it together in a trice. Her pink and white complexion, like that of so many Scots, disguised her age; she could be anywhere between fifty and eighty.

"Come in," said Mrs. Kenzie MacLarkie, and marched me through the hall into a parlor filled with shining Victorian furniture. With one exception it was all rather stiff: a faded, much laundered length of flannel covered the seat of a tufted chair by the hearth, and on the flannel napped a large ginger cat.

Cats reveal a great deal about their owners, I believe, more than dogs, which are naturally friendly. As an only child I'd always had cats of my own and learned what admirable and rewarding creatures they are. I wished Bart had liked them, but most men don't; Bart liked Labrador retrievers. Mrs. Kenzie's cat opened its tiger eyes as we entered and hailed us, so to speak, with a mighty stretch, all four feet extended sideways, then with a neat twist subsided on its back, front paws folded inward and hind paws splayed outward, revealing its downy pear-shaped belly, and there dozed comfortably off again. It was the display of a cat not only friendly, confident, and well-cared for, but with a sense of comedy. It takes a humorous human intelligence to bring out the humorous intelligence of cats, and that is why from the start I was not intimidated by the prim Mrs. Kenzie and her prim little house.

Mrs. Kenzie indicated the tufted sofa facing the hearth for me and seated herself opposite the cat. A Bible bristling with a variety of bookmarks occupied the round table next to her, and over the mantel hung a large sepia-toned photograph of a moustached man who, since the telephone listing was under the title of Mrs., must be the late Mr. Kenzie.

She waited for me to speak.

"It's kind of you to see me," I began. "You know, we Americans are very much interested in our ancestors on this side."

"It was your late husband's ancestors," she reminded me, "who came from this side, was it not?"

She sat with spine straight, hands folded, tiny stout black shoes barely touching the floor. She was reserved with me but not ill at ease. Her posture and her correctly phrased and faintly admonitory reply had the earmarks of a school-teacher.

"Yes," I told her, "but he always planned to come to Scotland himself when he could take the time." Her bright unwavering eyes only spurred me on to greater candor. "He was killed in an accident last winter, and I decided just as soon as I was able I'd come in his stead."

With a fractional glance she took in my crutch. "Aye, that is understandable." But her body didn't unbend. "Your late husband must have been descended from the MacLarkie who emigrated back in the nineties."

"You know of him, then?"

"Cair-tainly. Robert Barton MacLarkie. He later bought up most of the old laird's holdings. He was my husband's grandfather's first cousin."

"Then your husband and mine were distant cousins."

Her lips pursed. "Ver-r-ry distant."

"Well, there," I said, leaning back against the hard green velvet tufts, "that's the way everyone sounds when old Robert Barton MacLarkie's name comes up. I gather he was not well-liked."

"No-oo, he was not. Ye canna sairve God and Mammon."

"Do you think he did it for spite, buying up the old laird's holdings and then abandoning them?"

"It wasna done for charity."

"He bore the old laird a grudge, then?"

"He may have done. He was dismissed as a lad from the laird's sair-vice."

Now we were getting somewhere. "For what? For poaching?"

Her pale brows met in a peak and her mouth spread briefly in a grimace that wasn't really a smile. "Ye might call it that."

"Oho, Mrs. MacLarkie. How old was he at the time?"

"Old enough. Seventeen, they say."

"In other words, there was a lady involved."

I was aware in the last few minutes that her perfect poise was cracking. She broke out now, "Ye ask a quantity of questions, lass! Would ye like a cup o' tea? It would take me a wee minute just."

"No, thank you." I was hot in pursuit now and I wouldn't be diverted. "I would like to get to the bottom of this. There's a cloud over the MacLarkie name here, and since I have inherited Robert Barton's holdings I don't think it's unreasonable to want to know what caused this cloud and if possible make amends."

Then I saw pain in her eyes, like the laird's private sorrow. "Och, lass, ye canna make amends. It's over and done with."

"But it's not forgotten, is it? It does seem foolish to bear a grudge unto the third generation for someone's misbehavior nearly a hundred years ago, but perhaps that's all it takes for a feud to get started." (In high-principled Scotland, I added to myself.) "What did the old reprobate do — seduce the laird's lady?"

Immediately Mrs. Kenzie's spine, which had bent slightly a moment before, became ramrod straight again. "I do not take misbehavior lightly, Mrs. MacLarkie, whenever it happened."

Go to the foot of the class, Susan. "I'm sorry, I shouldn't have spoken facetiously. I suppose in a misguided way I was taking a stand for the MacLarkies."

"For your husband's side of the family," she reminded me again. She had moved forward in her chair and put her feet to the floor, ready to rise.

Oh dear. We were back on square one. We stared at each other, I pleading, she unyielding.

"Lass, I have said all I am going to say." The bright little eyes held a kind of pleading too, as though begging for release.

The interview was over.

I got my crutch under my arm and rose, so disappointed that for a moment I couldn't speak. Mrs. Kenzie promptly rose also, and her ginger cat awoke in a twinkling and leaped down to trot sociably along beside us, tail high.

I found my voice at the door. "Thank you for seeing me, anyway. I didn't mean to sound such a wrong note. I don't take misbehavior lightly either." A little picture of two people grappling in a chapel flashed uncomfortably in my mind. "Probably no one has dared cast aspersions on your side of the family, in your hearing at least."

"They have not." She opened the door with its oval glass panel. The ginger cat trotted out as though expecting us to follow, but since we did not he sat down and agreeably surveyed the garden. "My husband was a God-fearing man who lived all his life in Kirkangus and was much respected."

"So was mine, in California," I said. "Goodbye."

I stepped out onto the porch, and then felt her detaining touch on my sleeve. She barely came up to my shoulder. Her face was troubled; something about this impasse didn't sit well with her creed of charity. "No one should cast aspersions in your hearing either, lass. It was at the castle, was it not, that ye first heard them?"

"Yes. And since talking with you I marvel that I was allowed to set foot in the place."

"Och, that would be Jean's doing. She bears no grudge against anyone."

"You mean, it's only the present laird —" feeling strangely disloyal, I avoided mentioning his name, "who carries on the grudge?"

She swallowed, working the chords in her throat. She said at last, "If he does he has his reasons." Tears had sprung into her eyes. "I'll say no more. Good day." She stepped inside and softly shut the door.

From its vantage point on the porch the ginger cat saw me off, but I sensed more than one pair of eyes on my back as I went down the walk. I was pretty sure if I wheeled about I'd catch Mrs. Kenzie watching me unhappily from the glass panel.

II. . . .

Dottie was waiting in the car beyond the gate. I joined her and without a word she started the engine and drove up the curving High Street.

I sat in a crestfallen huddle for a while. I had uncovered the beginning of the feud, true enough, but I was convinced there was something more devastating, a crux, which no one could quite bring themselves to tell me − not Jock, or Jean, or little Mrs. Kenzie, although Mrs. Kenzie might have if I hadn't so crudely put her Presbyterian back up. Or would it have been too painful even so? It took more than a mild wrench, I was sure, to bring tears to her eyes.

I liked her, that's what made me feel so bad! I

would have liked being her friend, hearing her laugh, calling on her again with no purpose but enjoyment. Somewhere far afield there was a possible fondness for each other, I knew it in the way she said *lass*, I knew it from her ginger cat.

Perhaps Dottie would have remained tactfully silent if I hadn't exhaled a quick sigh.

"Struck out, didja?"

"Yes." We were mounting the hills above the town.

"This Mrs. MacLarkie antisocial?"

"No. But it was too upsetting for her to tell me what I want to know." I half-laughed. "And I don't even know what I want to know!"

"Sure you do. You want to know why MacLarkie's a dirty word around here."

I turned to her. "How did you guess that?"

"I didn't guess. I just keep my eyes and ears open. It goes with being paranoid."

I groaned. "Now, Dottie!"

She was thoughtful for a while and then she said, "The thing is, I'm trained to read a patient's face and eyes and walk and talk and even what she decides to wear, not just her temperature and blood pressure. And I knew something's got you revved up the last week or two, coupla times I bet your blood pressure's been *above* normal, if I coulda taken it. It's the

157

first time you've shown any real interest in life since I came on the scene, and same as Colin, nothing could make me gladder. All's I want for you is not to stub your toe, now that you're on your feet again."

"I'll try not to, Dottie —"

"Scotland's a romantic place, with these earls marching around in their pleated skirts, showing off their sexy legs."

As happens so often, she had me gulping halfway between laughter and indignation. "You think I'm falling in love!"

"Put it this way: you're come in a few times looking as if you'd had a shot of adrenalin. Each time it turns out you've been with his lordship."

"Dottie, it isn't possible to fall in love with someone when you're mourning a man like Bart!"

"Who says?"

"I says! Listen, Dottie. His lordship is a two-sided man, half hawk, half dove. He seems to be at war with himself, at least when I'm with him, and somewhere behind it all, I've perceived, is the name of MacLarkie. Or put it this way: the name of MacLarkie is an added aggravation to his problems; sort of like the last straw. I find this provocative. A challenge. Wouldn't it arouse *your* curiosity, if you were me? Yes, he *is* attractive in his Scottish getup, as Colin calls it; maybe he wears it defiantly, or pridefully, as part of a losing battle against the decline of his kind, or just because it's comfortable, but he wears it well because it's natural to him." I was clarifying my feelings out loud, I thought, but my voice sounded louder than it needed to be.

"Dottie," I continued more quietly, "he's quite another breed from Bart, who was one great, warmhearted man, with no buried booby traps, one whole person who never gave me anything but loving-kindness and protection." My voice dropped even lower. "How could I fall in love with a complicated, hostile stranger like Greggan after a perfect man like Bart?"

If Dottie had an answer she kept it to herself. I cleared my throat, calming down, and even though I'd minimized my attraction to Greggan I felt I'd regained a needed perspective.

We had come to the level moor and Dottie stopped the car. "Wanta take over?" We changed places. I found I did have the strength to apply the brakes, but the unaccustomed angle of pressure made my leg muscles ache. I drove the length of the moor, which seemed longer and wider without the mists shrouding it. Its heather-mottled outer reaches crept upward into golden foothills, and they in turn rolled back to the brownish-green snowcapped peaks. We were entirely alone in the sweeping emptiness. At the far end, before the drop to the loch, I turned the wheel over to Dottie again.

"Good exercise for you," Dottie said, as we descended. "And like I said before, I want you to make out on your own. If I should suddenly get sick or have an accident, you could get by."

"If you — what are you talking about? You never get sick or have accidents!"

"There's always a first time, right?"

I heard my own breath whistle in my throat as I sucked in my breath. "Dottie, are you suggesting someone might —"

"I'm not suggesting anything!" She drowned me out, almost yelling. "But if something should happen to me and I hadn't done my job, you could be helpless, and I can't allow that, is all. So now we're not gonna talk about it any more!" She changed the subject, dropping her voice, before I could put in another word. "About Lilah and Colin: we'll just tell them I wanted some wool and you wanted a driving lesson, right?"

"Right."

We both fell silent.

We had reached the loch-road. I felt a kind of creeping paralysis as we approached the castle on its promontory, as if succumbing to its brooding influence.

If someone wanted to get rid of me, they might believe it necessary to get Dottie out of the way first: was that what she was trying to tell me?

She had shaken me again. Fear stirred, and despite my resolution, particles of suspicion rose and flew about as before.

III. . . .

Colin insisted on sherry before lunch in the bar, and we picked up the festive mood where we'd left off last night. He looked very nice in a fisherman's sweater and jeans, not too mod for Scotland and not too square for an American.

As the bar emptied Jock came over to tell us there would be a *ceilidh*, pronounced caley, in Kirkangus Wednesday night and asked if we'd like to go.

"You might tell us what a *ceilidh* is," said Colin, "but she answer is yes, of course we'd like to go!"

Jock took up his bar-room or red-vested stance for imparting information, one hand on the back of a chair, one foot poised across the other, his bar cloth over his forearm. In the dining room he would impart the same information bending forward from the waist, hands clasped behind his back.

"A *ceilidh* is a get-together, or a dance, or a

songfest, or all three," he explained. "The drink flows freely more or less behind the scenes but it seldom turns into a *stramash*. A *stramash* is exactly what it sounds like. Jean and I are going if you'd like to make up a party." His eyes looked appealingly into mine. "I think you'd enjoy it."

"It sounds a bit — " began Lilah doubtfully.

"Delightful," cut in Colin, "and you and I, Lilah, shall do the Highland fling! How about you, Dottie?"

"Well, I got two left feet, but I'm game."

So it was arranged, and we moved on to the dining room for another animated meal, and then to the stairs for our quiet hour.

"Come for a walk with me, Susan, when you wake up," said Colin, before we separated. "I want her all to myself," he told Lilah and Dottie. "I haven't had a heart-to-heart talk with Susan in ages. In fact I don't think we've *ever* had one. I'll meet you downstairs in the hall, luv, at half-past three. Sweet dreams all!" He left us without waiting for me to say yes or no.

But I was glad to walk with him when the time came. After a while the musky odor of hearth fires catches in the lungs, the sheer weight of stonework, beams, and paneling becomes oppressive, and one needs to escape into the open air. We bundled up and went out through the courtyard to the causeway.

"Isn't it marvelous!" cried Colin, looking back at the towering pile of Strathburne. "Can you believe it's real? God, and the air, too — so cold and lonely: Scottish air! Everything's so majestic! I love it, don't you? I truly love it! I'm so glad I came!"

His enthusiasm refreshed me along with the air. I could leave my doubts and fears behind me for a while. He tucked his arm in mine and squeezed and did a little half-skip that almost made me lose my balance except that he had close hold of me. We giggled like children and moved on.

Partway down the loch-road he halted. "There!" he said, pointing to a ledge of stone on the green bank to our left. "We'll climb up there and dangle our legs and have a lovely view. It's only a short climb and I'll help you. Come on!"

We took it slowly and I grumbled and groaned, but we did at length arrive at the outcropping of rock and get ourselves seated. The drop below wasn't a frightening one, sloping gently downward, and the view had its somber beauty with its shades of bronze and green and faded purple. We could see the whole ascent from the opposite shore of fir-clad banks and foothills to the snow-dusted peaks. Colin's arm was again tucked under mine, for there was a penetrating chill despite our heavy clothing,

163

and we huddled shoulder to shoulder.

"I'm glad you've come, too, Colin."

"I'm glad you're glad. I take it from Lilah it's been a bit of a strain. Or is it just Lilah who's been a strain?"

"Ah, poor Lilah. No, it's no one's fault. The three of us made bad chemistry, that's all."

"What do you mean, poor Lilah?"

"She hasn't had much of a life. I hoped this would be fun for her."

"Oh, I don't know." Colin shrugged. "She's had a life in her own way. Andrew adored her."

"But somehow I have the impression he was a disappointment to her."

"Sweetheart, he was overshadowed by Bart. He had enough MacLarkie in his veins to try and outrival Bart, a mistake I never made, but of course he failed disastrously, especially in the field of high finance. Maybe Lilah wasn't so much disappointed in Andrew as resentful of Bart." Colin held his breath a second and then said, "She scares me a little. Does she scare you?"

I hesitated. "Well, sometimes. But mostly she tugs at my heart. Maybe she only scares me because she's not happy."

He threw back his head. "Oh, what a darling Susan-ish remark! You're not even sure what you meant, are you? But I am. You meant people who aren't happy usually have a lot of anger in them. That's what scares you." He hugged my arm. "You're a loving person, Susan, and loving people have a way of getting at the truth without a shred of meanness."

"Colin, you're always putting me in a favorable light."

"No." He was very emphatic, frowning at the view. "No, that's where you're wrong. I do *not* favor you. I see you as you are, or could be. You're the one who can't see yourself as you really are." He was even a little grim. "You've never been encouraged to."

"Oh, Colin —" I tried to draw away.

His arm held mine. "No, damn it, don't stop me. I'm going to finish. I loved Bart, too. No one looked up to Bart more than I did, from the time we were kids. *Everybody* looked up to Bart, literally and figuratively. He was overpowering and he overpowered you. He *blanketed* you in his all-encompassing, all-benevolent, perfectly self-satisfied love —"

"Colin!"

"Tell me this: did you ever quarrel? Did he ever say, 'You decide, Susan, you're much more discerning than I am?' Did you ever swim naked in the pool together in the middle of the night and —"

"Colin, stop!"

165

"I could have *cried* for you, you were so completely becalmed, so inert, so — unrealized! You barely had room to breathe! Did it never occur to you that Bart was insensitive, unimaginative —"

"Stop." I finally broke free of his arm. "Stop! I won't hear it. You are not to say another *word* against Bart to me, now or ever!"

"Yes. All right. I knew if I ever got started I'd go too far. I'm perfectly well aware I was jealous of him." His dark eyes smiled unrepentantly into mine. "I still am. But, see, now you're flashing with anger. I never saw you flash before. I wasn't sure you *could*. I don't care if you never speak to me again: at least you're alive, alive and glorious!"

His black brows were raised teasingly, and I was close enough to see the tiny shadows cast by the lashes on his shining lids. But there was gentleness in his look, and I couldn't hold onto my anger. I shut my eyes and exhaled a sharp breath. "Oh, Colin, really, what am I to do with you?"

He chuckled, and drew my shoulder close again. "Consider me your unregenerate brother. Bart always did."

"Do you ever think before you speak?"

"Why should I? What I speak *is* what I think. That way there's no mystery about me."

166

"Oh, but there is. There is about everyone, but especially the exceedingly artless."

"Ho ho! This new Susan is really rather alarming! I shall have to watch my step with you." He shivered. "Let's go back, shall we? My arse is freezing. I'm not wearing a fur-lined raincoat like you." He scrambled to his feet and pulled me up.

We strolled back as we had come, arm in arm. "What did you mean, Colin, when you said Lilah's had a life in her own way?"

He glanced out over the still loch. "I meant I believe Lilah has a very intense, very cool, pastel-colored, secret inner life. I don't dare guess what goes on in there but I bet if we knew we'd be astounded. And I believe she's more active in this spooky otherworld than she is in the real one, and I believe she's been at home in it since she was a child and always will be."

"Well!" I shivered too. "That does scare me!"

"Did she never scare you before your accident?"

He asked the question casually but I almost stopped in my tracks. And yet I was already on too familiar a basis with Colin not to answer him honestly, and perhaps honesty was the best tool with which to parry his clever artlessness. "I don't think so. But, Colin, if you're referring to the change in me since then, it was the accident itself that awakened me, not the removal of Bart from my life. It happens to people who come that close to death."

"You really haven't got over the trauma of it, have you?"

"I — am absorbing it, I hope."

"Even though you can't actually remember it?"

"I *can* remember it. It's what preceded it that I can't remember. Let's not talk about it, please."

"I don't want to talk about it. I don't want to talk about anything you don't want to talk about, including Bart. It wasn't true that I don't care if you never speak to me again. I do care, very much." He tilted back his head and breathed in the damp cold air. "Oh, Lord, Sue, even after that bountiful lunch I'm longing for tea! Do you get hot buttered scones?"

"Every day."

"Heavenly. I won't make you actually *run*, darling, but you can walk faster, can't you?"

Laughing, we stepped out smartly.

Lilah was waiting for us over the tea tray in the lounge.

"Where's Dottie?" I asked.

"I don't know." Lilah's eyes held a little blur of anxiety. "I knocked on her door before

I came down but there was no answer. Maybe she has a headache."

A curious tingling passed upward over my arms and neck, ending in my scalp. I said, as unconcernedly as possible, "I want to go upstairs anyway before tea. I'll check on her. You two go ahead, and I'll be down in a minute."

I mounted the stairs faster than I knew I was able. I went through the connecting door between our bedrooms, which was never locked. She lay on her bed, her mouth open. I shook her. I couldn't rouse her.

IV. . . .

Dr. Craigie appeared at last in the door of the waiting room. Colin had stepped outside for a cigarette ("Visitors Are Requested to Refrain from Smoking"), and I sat alone under the yellow ceiling light looking at copies of the ubiquitous *Reader's Digest* and *The Scots Magazine*, my eyes registering nothing from one page to another. We had been waiting in the Kirkangus hospital clinic for over an hour.

Dr. Craigie must often have seen that blind terrified stare transferred from *The Scots Magazine* to his face: Have you, O Champion, won this match with Death?

"She'll do," he said, as he'd said once of me, and relief surged from my chest to the back of my eyes and my face crumpled as if it didn't belong to me; the rush produced a cough, not quite a sob, and then I controlled myself. But I couldn't speak.

He sat down beside me, giving off hospital scents and the odor of pipe tobacco, and spoke just above a whisper. "We've pumped her out and administered antagonists, and her respiration has improved. Fortunately she didn't take a lethal dose."

He had come promptly to the castle in response to Jean's urgent summons. Searching Dottie's medicine cabinet he'd found the vial of Demerol. He hadn't waited for the Kirkangus ambulance but with Colin's help had carried Dottie down the back stairs and into his car. I rode with her, and Colin followed in my car.

"We'll keep her here a day or two," Craigie continued, "but all the signs indicate continued improvement. She's out of the coma and asking for you. But before you see her I'd like to ask you, has she been depressed lately, would you say?"

"Dr. Craigie, I'm certain she didn't take an overdose on purpose!" I kept my voice low, like his, as if we were in church, although there was no one else in the waiting room. "She had the Demerol on hand for *me*. She nursed me after an automobile accident and it was prescribed for me when I was in pain and couldn't sleep. I haven't needed it for a long time but she brought some of my medications along on our trip just in case. No, she wasn't depressed, she's not at all the depressive type! She does have migraines once in a while and takes aspirin for them. She must have taken the Demerol by mistake; the tablets look very much alike."

"It's not a mistake a nurse would make."

I turned my face away. "I know." I was pulling at my hands the way Lilah does, I realized, and stopped immediately. Does Lilah do it when she is evasive, as well as anxious? I said, "I suspect Dottie's headaches are due to her needing glasses, at least for reading and fine work, but she's stubborn and doesn't like me to mention it. Don't you think, in the weak light over the medicine cabinet . . ." I swallowed. "Or she might have accidently put away a tablet in her aspirin bottle . . ." My voice trailed away. I knew I didn't sound very convincing, but I wanted to believe myself.

Could Dottie have taken the dose on purpose? To increase her hold on me? Making me aware of my need for her by removing herself suddenly. Casting suspicion on someone else? The idea was preposterous. I loathed myself for thinking such a thing.

Dr. Craigie considered the matter with his

arms folded like a conscientious juryman. He said at last, "Perhaps she'll be able to explain it to you later." He unfolded his arms. "I'll take you in to her." He stood up. "You mustn't stay but a wee moment."

I rose, too. "Dr. Craigie, don't let her come home too soon. Keep her awhile, even if you have to tie her down."

He smiled. "She's the vigorous type, is she? That's promising. Your brother-in-law had better take you home after you visit her or you'll miss your supper. If there's any change, we'll let you know." He led the way to Dottie's room.

My heart stopped a second at first sight of her. She looked as if she'd been in a fight, and indeed she had. Her lips were bruised, probably from the stomach pump, her hair was matted and the skin around her eyes darkened. She appeared to be unconscious, her mouth sagging, but the instant I touched her, her eyes opened and she recognized me with a faint curl of her swollen lips. Dr. Craigie hovered nearby, and a young nurse was stationed on the far side of the bed.

"Toldja," croaked Dottie, slurring her words, her eyes unfocused. "Toldja, didn' I?"

"Oh, Dottie," I whispered, holding tight to her hand. I couldn't argue with her now.

"Who brought . . . who . . . ?"

"We brought you in Dr. Craigie's car. Colin followed." And I added, guessing it was what she wanted to hear, "I made Lilah stay behind."

"Good. Don't . . . don't . . ." She struggled to form words.

"I won't." I guessed, too, that she wanted to tell me not to ride with Lilah, and I loathed myself again for guessing. My forehead was clammy. Dr. Craigie watched her, frowning.

"Lock . . . door . . ."

"Dottie, don't worry."

"Promise!"

"I promise. Please don't worry about anything. Just get well."

"By Jes's, better b'lieve . . . Careful, kiddo . . . careful." She closed her eyes. Dr. Craigie signaled me to go now.

I left.

Colin was waiting for me in the visitor's room. "Okay, Susan?"

"Okay."

"Thank God." He pressed my hand. "I'll take you home."

My face must have told him I was nearly spent, and mercifully he asked no questions, but got me to the car and concentrated on driving over unfamiliar roads in the dark. I slumped in my seat, my eyes shut.

Jean came out from behind her desk to meet

me, and Munro and Severn gathered around. At the sound of my voice Lilah hurried out of the lounge, followed by the Barsington-Bankses. Lady Fanquill floated up from nowhere.

I gave them the good news, and they murmured their thankfulness. Major Barsington-Banks said, "Rum!" I couldn't quite look Lilah in the eye.

I asked Jean if I could have a tray sent to my room. There was nothing I wanted so much as to crawl into bed.

"I'll see to it at once." Jean's eyes were full of commiseration. "Go on up. Oh, I almost forgot. My dad sent you this."

She went behind her desk and came out again with a cane, a hand-worked stick of burled wood, the color of honey, light but strong as steel. For one awful moment I thought I was going to disintegrate into sobs. In my overwrought state it moved me inordinately that Greggan had remembered about the cane.

Then I felt my misery fall away. After all, Dottie was going to get well. It was a different world!

I handed Colin my crutch and took up the cane.

"It becomes you," said Lady Fanquill.

Lilah started forward. "I'll go up with you, dear."

"No." But I didn't recoil. I was calm and firm. "Stay and have a drink with Colin. I'd rather be by myself. I don't need help. Watch me!"

I twirled the cane like Charlie Chaplin and took a few splayfooted steps as I left them. Perhaps they too were balanced precariously between anguish and relief; they all laughed.

I am safe, I feel confident, for tonight. Two "accidents" in one day would start people asking questions. Even so, my door is bolted; so is Dottie's.

I agree with Craigie: Dottie is too good a nurse to have opened the vial of Demerol by mistake. Even a blind man can tell the difference between a vial and a bottle.

I am taking no more chances.

Around eleven there was a soft knock, Lilah's knock, but I pretended I was asleep.

CHAPTER 9

I. . . .

I slipped away early this morning, down the back stairs. The cane was a great improvement. Greggan had chosen just the right height and weight, and it was far less cumbersome than the crutch. All I need now is the feeling of security, rather than the actual support.

Poor Greggan, I thought, rounding the drive-way to the garage sheds — torn once more, no doubt, by remorse, offering amends in the shape of a cane!

And then, although I was smiling, something quite serious collected within me and presented itself: I did not wish him to suffer anything, least of all these agonies of conscience.

Whatever the makeup of his ambivalence toward me, I wished him free of it. I knew of his concern for the welfare of others, I knew of his love for his daughter and hers for him, I was convinced of his essential decency. It wasn't fair that his life — past ordeals aside — should contain torment now.

And my capricious attraction to him changed in that moment from one form to another, an advancement like the metamorphosis of worm to winged creature, from unreasoning desire, sexual and self-realizing, to something almost as objective, as distant from self, as altruism; at least to a recognition of him more kindly, more compassionate, more relinquishing, than any emotion I'd had for him before. I preferred his peace to my own gratification.

There was gravity in this new feeling, akin to sadness but lacking in self-pity, like saying good-bye to someone you loved but whom you knew must go, would be happier gone. Love? But I wouldn't take up the word. The name of the new feeling was not important.

I hoped this was a betterment that would last, and not a glimpse of an ideal I couldn't live up to.

I backed the car out of its niche without difficulty, puttered forward along the drive skirting the castle wall, and headed down the ramp toward the bridge.

As if to put me to the test at once, Greggan was there, on the stone wharf below the bridge, untying his skiff. It was a good day for fishing, dull again and windless. I stopped the car and rolled down the window. He looked up without smiling or changing his rather blank, preoccupied expression.

"Thanks to your cane," I said, "I no longer hobble." I didn't need to raise my voice in the gray stillness, but it sounded foreign to me, remote, a clear calm outdoor voice.

He stared at me as if I'd spoken in Hindustani. After a long pause he answered noncommittally, "Very well then."

"It was thoughtful of you and I greatly appreciate it."

The blue eyes continued to stare; or looked without seeing. He grasped the skiff's painter but his hands were motionless. Were the two sides of his nature at this moment locked in combat? He said, his voice subdued but carrying over the gray air and water, "I haven't seen you drive before. I didn't know you were up to it." Down-to-earth remarks, free apparently of inner discord, far removed from our last frenzied encounter; yet the eyes looked haunted.

"I don't know if I'm up to it or not," I told him quietly, "but I'm going to find out." Don't be afraid, the quiet voice was saying, I will never again disrupt your creed of honor.

"Your nurse Mrs. O'Halloran is better?"

"She is expected to improve."

He bowed his head for a moment to rub the back of his neck, a thought-collecting rub.

"Jean tells me you want someone to show you your holdings."

"Yes. When I receive Mr. MacBaine's map."

An extraordinary conversation, he below the bridge and I above it, a conversation so perfunctory yet made intimate by the autumnal hush over the loch, made melancholy by the renunciation of feelings; a disembodied conversation.

He said, shifting his stance at last, as if preparing to take to his boat, "No one knows your land better than I do. I need no map, but probably you would like to have it on hand. When you receive it, will you let me show you about?" He added, and God knows what it cost him in pride, "There will be no contention, on my word."

"Certainly." I wished to leave him suddenly. "I'll let you know when the map comes. Goodbye." I raised my cane in a solemn flourish and drove on.

As I reached the loch-road my eyes filled with tears. They didn't surprise me. I blinked them away, cleared my throat, and didn't look back.

II. . . .

They told me at the hospital that Dottie was much better but having a wee nap, so I left word I'd be back in an hour, and drove off down the street to the post office. My legs were going through the old car-driving motions with less stiffness.

"Murdo MacLarkie?" The stout white-haired postmistress in black coverall eyed me curiously. "Och, he lives out beyond Gladdoch Glen. The road goes by his cottage." She gave me directions. She wanted to detain me, I sensed, and she watched me leave with an odd expression, almost apprehensive, which I tried to shrug off as I returned to my car.

I drove straight through town, past the blazing dahlias, past Mrs. Kenzie MacLarkie's rowans, and out eventually into a long narrow valley between mountains, the Gladdoch Glen. It was another one-lane road with passing bays, and I pulled in for one or two cars, but soon I was out of the Glen and on a ridge overlooking grazing land with no living thing in sight save the sheep with their staring senseless eyes.

Murdo MacLarkie did indeed live in an outlying district. I could see the stone cottage from a mile away, huddled with its byre and sheeppens under the lee of the ridge. No smoke rose from the chimney, not a soul or creature moved in the yard.

I drew the car off the road, got out and walked with my cane down the gravel track to the house, and knocked on the door. No one answered. The damp windless air seemed to listen with me. The place seemed deserted. Not a flower nor shrub nor tree relieved the barrenness of it.

"Hello!" I called.

And then a dog uttered a single muffled bark beyond the house, a bark that ended at once in a yelp, and I followed the sound, stepping around the house to the shed, or byre. "Hello!" I called again. The dog gave another half-bark, as though someone held its muzzle, and there was a scuffle within the byre, and then again silence. I stood uncertainly in the space between house and byre. "Mr. MacLarkie!"

The hair on the back of my scalp prickled. I knew someone lurked behind that shed door, restraining the dog, whose nails skidded on the wooden flooring. I didn't like this place, remote from a neighborly world, I didn't like its total lack of beauty, its muzzled dog. I felt sure I was being watched through a crack in the door.

I turned about and started quickly back to the car.

"What did y'want?"

The sly voice made me start and suck in my breath. I've no doubt it was meant to do that. I wheeled about. The shed door had opened and the man stood in the shadows grasping the

181

dog's snout between viselike fingers. The man was tall and thin, dressed in black, or gray worn to black, and his thick unkempt hair was a dusty orange, his face spattered with brown freckles. But it was his eyes, yellow and slightly opaque like sheep's eyes, that shocked me, and involuntarily I took a step backward. I had never seen such eyes.

"You're — Murdo MacLarkie?"

"Aye." His lips were parted to show brown teeth, a grimace that may have been meant to be a smile but which seemed only menacing.

"I — I was looking up my husband's relatives in Scotland. I'm sorry if I disturbed you —"

I know now with hindsight that I had walked into a trap, but at the time I felt only that I was in the presence of evil. I took another step backward. The dog, whimpering, struggled to free itself.

"I disown my relatives," the man said, staring in his all-encompassing way, "or they disown me. It is agreeable on both sides." He broke into a terrible cackling, bending and bringing his hands to his knees, as if he were suffering some kind of seizure. In so doing he released the dog, which fled like a streak, vanishing behind the shed. The seizure ended abruptly and the man straightened and came forward out of the byre.

I fell back, gripping my cane across my waist

with both hands. "Well," I answered, my breath short, "I only thought – I looked up the MacLarkies in the telephone book – I won't trouble you further –" I edged sideways to the corner of the house.

He advanced inexorably in a straight line, his eyes, too, focused straight ahead. He was blind.

It struck me when he didn't change direction as I moved sideways. The wide cloudy eyes were blind!

"Stay!" he said, grinning, "stay! Ye're young, are ye? A pretty young girl? It may be I can help ye. Yer disowned MacLarkie has something to offer!" And swiftly, grinning at the wall of the house before him, his grimy clawlike fingers unzipped his fly and groped in the dark recess within.

Stifling gasps of horror, I turned and moved as fast and as soundlessly as I could, around the house, up the gravel track, back to the car. Oh God, I cried in silence, let the engine start! I couldn't look back but I was aware of the dark shadow coming around the corner of the house. The engine started. The gravel flew under my wheels. A spasm of cackles followed me.

I drove a mile or two straight on, bleating, "Jesus God!" like Dottie O.

I realized eventually I'd have to turn around and retrace my route. Would Murdo be posted by the side of the road, saluting me as I passed with his badge of manhood? I went by the house at seventy miles an hour. But there was no one in sight, no man, no dog. The place looked deserted again.

I raced on over hill and dale and only when I'd left the heathery glen behind and come within sight of the first houses of Kirkangus did I slacken speed and catch my breath.

"So much for Murdo MacLarkie," I said, and burst into wild laughter. "Struck out again, kiddo."

III. . . .

Dottie did look better, though still very pale. We were alone in the hospital room. Before I could open my mouth she demanded to know, "Who brought you?"

"Nobody. I drove myself."

"I'll be damned." She sounded more like her old self. "See, it was a good thing you tried it out with me. From now on don't let *anybody* drive you. Where'd you get the nifty cane?"

"The laird sent it to me, by way of Jean."

"Huh. Smart guy. He must've noticed you were ready to graduate from the crutch. Nice."

"Dottie, you're not sitting up yet. How do you feel?"

"Better. I hoped to come home today but I'm

184

still too woozy. Sitting up makes me nauseated. I'd be more of a hindrance to you than a help. Doc says maybe I can leave Thursday but I already made up my mind it'll be tomorrow."

"Since when have you ever disobeyed doctors' orders?"

"Yeah, well, they like to tack on a day or two for good measure. This Craigie is watching me for signs of depression," she looked downward as she straightened the fold of her sheet, "but you know and I know somebody slipped me a Mickey Finn."

"Do we?" I whispered. "Do we know?"

"If you don't, I do. Somebody put Demerol in my aspirin bottle. Not to kill me, that would cause too much of a hullabaloo, the police might have to look into it and all, but they sure as hell wanted to get me out of the way. A few Demerol would do the trick, especially to someone who wasn't used to taking it. If it'd been you I was giving aspirin to – even aspirin – I'd have carried it to the light and looked carefully, but for me, well, I just shook three or four pills out of the bottle and popped them in my mouth. One hundred milligram tablets of Demerol do look a lot like aspirin. What makes me mad at myself is, I felt in my bones something was brewing, there was just too much sweetness and light. Okay, so you found me in time. So who was it made you anxious, made you go find me?"

"It was Lilah. That doesn't necessarily mean anything!"

"All right, I'll go on saying *they*. *They* wanted me to be found. They didn't know when I'd take the Demerol but they were pretty sure I'd take it sooner or later because they know I take aspirin for migraines, and they knew I'd survive it and no one would try to prove it wasn't a mistake. *Somebody* is very patient and determined. Now, look. Don't tell anybody I'm coming home tomorrow, or Thursday, not even Jean. Let them think I'll be here the rest of the week."

"Why?"

"So they'll think they've got plenty of time. So I can get back there before —" She stopped.

"Before what?" The skin on my forearms had contracted.

She looked me in the eye. "Before they go after *you*."

"Dottie, for *God's* sake!" I brought both fists down on each side of my knees, thumping the padded seat of my chair. But I was whispering. "What are you trying to do to me?"

"I'm trying to scare the hell out of you."

I stared at her.

"So that you'll be *careful*, you woodenhead — *extra* careful!"

"But — 'go after me'! *Why?* What ever for?"

"Mon-ey, kiddo, mon-ey. What is it ever for? The root of all evil. Your husband's money would go to the surviving relative, wouldn't it?"

"Yes, but if I die, Colin would inherit!"

"Something would happen to Colin, too, that could never be explained. Have you ever wondered about Andrew and his heart attack? Maybe *he* didn't get medical attention in time, as I did. Okay, if you're not scared, I am!" In her anxiety Dottie had raised her head, but now she dropped back, her face very white.

I stood up and took her hand. As reassuringly as possible I told her, "I *am* scared. I've been scared a long time. I promised you last night and I promise you now: I will be extra careful. There. Now rest, Dottie, and don't worry."

She said wearily, "One murder is enough."

"One *murder?* You mean —"

"I mean Bart MacLarkie."

CHAPTER 10

Stunned, I sat in my car outside the hospital. If Dottie had set out to influence me, to convert me at last to paranoia, she had succeeded.

True, I had considered the possibility of someone's tampering with the brake fluid before Bart and I left the house. True, I'd had ever-increasing misgivings, and had begun to abhor the word *accident* . . .

But I had never used or heard anyone else use the word *murder*.

I couldn't go back to the castle now, not while *murder* sat in the forefront of my mind. I went in search of a hairdresser, and found one upstairs over a coffee shop. A shy, whispering girl gave me a shampoo and set, and I closed my eyes and gave myself up to her soothing hands. Under the dryer I had British women's magazines to occupy me, and when I descended to the street I found that the brief respite had done its pacifying work and my appetite had returned.

I went into the coffee shop, not overly clean but serving a good soup, (the wonderful soul-warming soups of Scotland must have been invented as an antidote to the climate), and a passable omelette.

Then I located the local library, where I made one last attempt to dig out the facts about the MacLarkies. The available reference volumes were concerned with the illustrious and the titled, and the MacLarkie name didn't appear at all.

However, while I was about it I decided I might as well look up the earls of Strathburne, and I settled down at the reading table to piece together their history. They had figured in every border clash and uprising since the beginning of time, from Bannockburn and Flodden Field to Culloden Moor, and I even came across a few illustrations showing blond Alisdairs and Hughs in full Highland regalia with a warlike gleam in their eyes and plenty of *sgian dubhs* and claymores stashed about them. But as rebellion in Scotland declined, so did the record of the earldom dwindle. The present Lord Greggan, Hugh Malcolm Alisdair, was mentioned in his father's half inch of abbreviated biography as having been born in 1930, but there the, reference ended. The volume was published in 1947.

I rose to inquire about something more up-to-date when I noticed the day was fading and the bespectacled male librarian was eyeing me in a closing-time way.

Murder.
The word was waiting for me as I emerged into the open air; it pounced and dropped on me.

Head down, I made my way to my car, parked farther along the curb. The street was nearly empty, the shops were closing. A nocturnal scent of autumn stole down from the hills with the descent of dusk.

I came alongside my car. Something moved behind it. I halted. A figure rose up. I opened my mouth in a soundless scream.

"It's only me, Mrs. MacLarkie. Gordon Thornhill."

Now I knew what inroads terror had made in one day. If I hadn't been so preoccupied with *murder*, I'd have noticed the little red sports car parked behind mine. He approached me, coming around to the curb. He looked so normal, so smartly dressed and eager and harmless, that my lungs eased and my pounding heart slowed.

"Sorry I startled you — Susan. May I call you

Susan when I'm off duty? I knew you'd driven to town alone so I looked about for you before I returned to the castle for the evening shift. Wouldn't you like me to follow you home? Or if you'd rather not drive in the dark, I can run you home in my car and arrange for someone to bring yours along after us."

"Oh, I can drive all right, Gordon, thank you."

"I wish there were time to buy you a drink."

"I'll have one at the castle. I could use one."

"Aye, but if you were to say the word, I'd throw everything over — bar, dining room, castle, and all, for an hour alone with you. I try not to cast sheep's eyes at you when I'm on duty but it demands the most rigorous and exhausting self-discipline."

I shook my head. "Poor Gordon." I was beginning to laugh.

He sighed. "I love my country, my multifarious family, and the assurance of the future as castle deputy, but when a guest like yourself descends on us from the outer world there is a noticeable drop in my self-satisfaction."

"You mean, this happens fairly frequently?" I teased.

But Gordon is a practiced banterer. "No one so beautiful happens frequently," he replied, with an attempt at solemnity, "in this world or any other. Ah well, at least I shall hold you in my arms tomorrow night."

I had moved toward my car, but turned, startled.

"With scores of people looking on." He grinned. "At the *ceilidh*." He opened my car door for me.

I found I was glad to have someone following me. The upland moor was deserted in the gloaming, with a ghastly beckoning emptiness, still as death.

Murder.

I couldn't escape the word. It seemed to form a knot in my brain, cutting off all previous rationality like a tourniquet. Optimism, trust, a predisposition toward affection, all became tendencies of the past. The word served as a dividing point, a severance: on the one side hope, on the other horror.

I had come to believe it: *My husband was murdered.*

II. . . .

It was nearly six when we returned, and Gordon hurried off to open the bar. Jean was still on duty. She gave me my mail, including a fat envelope from the firm of MacBaine and Atherton, and asked me about Dottie.

I told her Dottie was better, and then Jean

leaned forward. The hall was empty. "Susan," she said quietly, "I just wanted to say, I wanted you to know, if you are worried in any way, and there is anything I can do to help, you have only to ask me." She straightened at once and gave me a quick smile, as if to tell me she might not be as anxious as she sounded, in case there was nothing to be anxious about.

A kind word moves me more readily to tears than an unkind one, but tonight tears, too, had dried up. I could only think, Even Jean suspects something is wrong! I felt I had a true friend in Jean, and of all the people who might have ulterior motives where I was concerned, including Dottie, including Gordon, even Greggan, Jean was purely well-meaning. But I couldn't confide in her. What could I pick out of the chaos of my imaginings to tell her? I felt almost like a carrier of disease; I didn't wish to contaminate our friendship. I made a smile. "If there is anything I can ask of you, I'll ask."

"Ask," she echoed with a breath. She stepped back.

"Wait," I said. I opened the envelope from MacBaine and glanced through the documents. "Our friend Archibald has sent my papers, including a map. Your father offered to show me my property when the map arrived."

Her smile brightened. "I'll tell him it's come,"

she answered. She looked so pleased that I wondered if she did, after all, have ulterior motives.

There wasn't time for a drink with Gordon before changing for dinner, so I slipped upstairs.

Chrissie, our maid, had been in to make up my room, of course, after I left in the morning, but I made a careful check for signs of tampering by a subsequent intruder. No one with any sense, I thought, not even with a murderous obsession, would repeat the same method of attack within twenty-four hours, but I'd promised myself to take no chances. I emptied the water carafe and rinsed it, examined my toothpaste and brush and even my makeup. Everything seemed to be in order.

I felt a little foolish.

I can look Lilah in the eye now. I am not intimidated by her in the old way, when she had the power, knowingly or not, to make me feel guilty.

The word *murder* not only dries up tears, not only severs, but reverses.

Lilah and Colin were just sitting down to dinner when I joined them. They immediately inquired about Dottie, and Lilah asked when she was coming home. From being one who floundered over a falsehood, I now can lie. I told them probably not until the end of the week.

We started our soup, and I asked how they had spent the day.

Colin had explored the castle and enjoyed a marvelous talk with Dougal the gamekeeper. "Although, frankly, I didn't understand a word he said. I *think* we were talking about deer stalking."

Lilah had worked on her needlepoint and napped as usual. Her big pale eyes lifted appealingly. "I still hope, Susan, that you'll find an afternoon to go exploring with me. I discovered a pretty road Sunday at the other end of the loch, but it isn't much fun, looking at a beautiful view alone." Then she laughed at herself. "Listen to me! Poor little Lilah!"

Colin answered her before I could speak. "You'd better get used to the fact that Susan is now independent. She can walk unassisted — except for the laird's darling cane — and she can drive. Tomorrow night at the *ceilidh* she'll discover she can dance. From now on we're not going to see Susan for dust."

Lilah smiled. "And I'm all for it! I often wished, even before — Bart died, that Susan would assert herself more."

It was a singular thing for Lilah to say, but it

was the tiny pause like an inaudible hiccough, before she uttered Bart's name, that I fastened on. I knew there was no hatred in my eyes as I looked at her because I felt none — only dullness, only numbness, and somewhere in the background, still distantly pulsating beyond the cutoff point, pity.

Colin, as is his habit, filled in the gap caused by my silence. He was in a mischievous mood tonight. "That's what I've been trying to tell Susan. I wished she'd *express* herself, let alone assert herself. I don't mean shout Bart down, no one could, he had too big a voice, but once in a while come out quietly with a 'Shove it, love,' or 'Bullshit, dearest' —"

"Colin!" Lilah reproved. "I do draw the line at vulgarity!"

"Do you, dear?" His black eyes sparkled. "But didn't you ever wish, when the MacLarkie brothers were gathered together and being their most jovial and noisy and overwhelming — didn't you ever wish you could tell them, 'Drop dead'?"

There was a little throbbing halt.

"How can you say such thing?" Lilah gasped.

He patted her hand. "Because I'm like a bad conscience, always saying things nobody wants to hear. They pop out before I can stop myself. I wish you'd teach me how to keep my wicked thoughts to myself."

That made matters worse. Lilah was about to retort, when his implication struck her; she caught her breath, and was speechless.

"Colin," I said, "shove it."

He fell back in his chair and burst into laughter. Even Lilah, after a moment, joined in.

I left them after coffee. The Barsington-Bankses were making up a game of bridge, and since Lilah plays well, and Colin can turn his hand to or bluff his way through almost any social skill, it was my opportunity to bow out.

I went upstairs, locked my doors, and made another check of my room. I changed for the night and sat down at my desk with my journal.

But as I began to recount the morning my pen slowed and stopped, and I became lost in the remembered atmosphere of flat calm, the pervading quiet of air and water, the limbo of suspended emotion when Greggan and I conversed by the bridge. My wish for his peace of mind was still firm, and brought me peace as well.

My thoughts were interrupted by a knock, not as tentative as Lilah's. I called out to ask who was there.

It was Severn. I unlocked my door. At sight of me in a negligee he reddened with both sets of blushes and fastened his eyes determinedly on mine. "For you, mistress!" He thrust an envelope in my hand and fled.

The handwriting was vigorous, rather like Old English script, and there was a small red crest at the top of the gray paper. The message consisted of a single sentence.

If it is convenient for you, I will pick you up at two o'clock tomorrow to view your estate.

It was signed simply, *Greggan.*

CHAPTER 11

I. . . .

I slept heavily. Perhaps the remembered limbo helped. If anyone tried my door in the night, I was oblivious of it.

In the morning Jean gave me a bouquet of roses for Dottie, and I left for Kirkangus without having seen Lilah or Colin. They keep to themselves in the morning, I know, but I slunk away even so, and didn't realize until I was on the loch-road that I'd been holding my breath.

There was time only for a short visit with Dottie before her early lunch arrived, and Dr. Craigie was present part of the time.

"Ran *one degree* of temperature last night," wailed Dottie, "so he's gotta keep me here another day!"

"We'll not have you leave while there's any danger of respiratory infection," said Craigie quietly. There was still a look of perplexity in his eyes. "As a nurse you must understand that." He turned to consult with the imposing matron who accompanied him. Dottie rolled her eyes helplessly behind his back.

After he departed she lay back, resigned. She wasn't yet her apple-cheeked self and she knew it. I assured her all was well with me, gave her the roses from Jean, which pleased her, and as the probationer arrived with her tray, left her.

I debated about going again to the coffee shop, but decided to go back to the castle for lunch. There seems to me less risk in acting as if I suspect nothing than in letting it be known I'm on my guard and starting a cat and mouse game. But I drove home more slowly than I'd gone the other way.

Among the bills and business letters from the States waiting for me at the desk was a smaller envelope with a Kirkangus postmark. The handwriting was fine and uniform, just what one would expect from a lady who kept an immaculate house, or who might once have been a schoolteacher.

Dear Madam, it said. *It lies heavy on my conscience that I let you go away as I did. Pride goeth before a fall and I have resolved to put mine in my pocket. Come back and have a cup of tea with me and I will try to be more hospitable. Sincerely, Margaret MacLarkie.*

I smiled for the first time today. She promised

nothing, but I thought her letter promising.

Colin must have sensed a little variety was needed in our daily routine, and persuaded a gaunt, lone Canadian, Wilbur Grant, to join us at lunch. On holiday from one of the off-shore oil companies, Wilbur Grant is a geologist, and looks it, with a fissured face and long stratified frame. And like many professionals with but a single interest, he was articulate on his subject, and we learned throughout lunch a great deal that was fascinating, to me at least, about the prehistoric upheavals that made Scotland so uneven.

Lilah was quiet and wide-eyed throughout, perhaps abstracted. I tried not to dwell on her, wondering what was going on in her mind, but when I felt her eyes on me I could look back at her composedly; whereupon she gave me her wistful look with her funny smile. Once upon a time I'd have reached out and squeezed her hand, and I missed those days; now I turned away.

By the end of the meal Colin had changed the conversation from heavy to light, and I looked at my watch and found it was nearly two o'clock. I excused myself, saying I had an appointment.

"Don't squander your strength, darling," said Colin, with a glint of deviltry in his eyes. Had my face given me away? "Remember, you're going to dance tonight!"

I hurried upstairs to change into stouter shoes.

As I came down again I saw Lady Fanquill emerging from the lounge. We halted, facing each other outside the empty bar. I was aware then that we share something, this vaporous lady and I, something like a secret but without substance, a tenuous understanding, greater in unspoken form than spoken. And I felt that in a sense she knows me better than I know myself, as though she has telepathic access to all information.

I was suddenly not in a hurry, waiting for her to speak.

She usually begins with a question. "You will be warm enough?"

She certainly has access to information about the castle's daily goings-on, at least. If not the castle spy, she is the castle clairvoyant. I assured her I would be warm enough.

"You have much to go through, have you not, my dear?"

This time she dumbfounded me.

"I wish I possessed a talisman to give you," she continued. "I can only give you my respect and affection."

"That is more than enough," I told her,

deeply touched. "And surely, with your nephew, I shan't need a talisman."

She shook her head slowly. "I wish you would not be too sure." She pressed my hand, then withdrew and moved to the stairs.

II. . . .

The battered Land Rover was drawn up in the courtyard, and as I came out Greggan broke off a parley with Munro and they helped me into the high passenger's seat. Greggan marched about to his side of the car and climbed in, and we set off at once. He wore over his kilt a jacket with patches on the elbows, and he had flung a stolelike wool plaid over one shoulder, for extra warmth perhaps, or in case of rain.

I was still disconcerted by Lady Fanquill's final admonition, and it was Greggan who spoke at last. "It's selfish of me, appointing myself your guide." We were trundling along the causeway. "I've a wish to go over the old estate."

I answered something to the effect that I was glad the tour served a purpose for him as well as for me, and after a quick glance to make sure I wasn't practicing veiled sarcasm he settled into silence. If he wanted it understood he was conducting the tour for his sake rather than mine, I could in my state of relinquishment allow him to score the point. If I needed a talisman against him, as Lady Fanquill seemed to think I might, perhaps this neutrality constituted one.

I wondered if Lady Fanquill had in mind the fact that I alone stood between Lord Greggan and his "old estate." But I couldn't take her caution seriously; I couldn't rouse myself to believe I was this afternoon in peril. Maybe I was becoming case-hardened. Maybe my mistrust had become so generalized that I no longer needed to add anyone to my list, so wearisome that I no longer bothered.

A pale watery sunlight filtered through the overcast and the flood of air rushing at us through the open windows of the car was bracing. We headed down the loch-road and kept straight on past the turn for Kirkangus.

"Is that Craggy Head?" I asked, peering up at the sheer stone face looming over the end of the loch.

"Yes," he answered.

All right, if he didn't care for conversation I could be quiet, too. It was no longer my business to figure out his moods.

I kept my eyes on the banks of the green hills with their clumps of fir and their white specks of sheep grazing, and I felt a fleeting pang of loneliness, as if I'd had a premonition I might never see these hills again, as if I knew if I lived I would be homesick for them, for this stringent air, for this sane, rugged reality. "You have much to go through," my seeress-friend had told me. Perhaps she had foreseen this heartache.

If I lived — again, like a Freudian slip, a latent thought had surfaced. My conscious mind received it from my unconscious without surprise. I must have been preparing for the possibility without knowing it. Even in the hospital in California when my life hung in the balance, I'd never been so soberly fatalistic. Had Lady Fanquill warned me against myself?

Greggan all at once drew the vehicle to a halt. The paved road had dwindled to a dirt track. He took up the map, which I'd placed open in the space between us. "We are crossing now," he said, pointing out a line in the southwest corner, "from my land into yours."

And quite apart from the somber workings of my brain, my heart awoke with a leap and began to beat jubilantly. Now, at last, I was completing my pilgrimage! I thought of Bart, hoping he knew in his impervious distance that I had found his patch of Scotland.

We traveled on over the narrow track into a cleft between overhanging ledges. Firs and giant ferns almost met overhead. The cut widened slightly and we drove alongside a rocky stream into which burns cascaded. It was a place of deep shadow and dense humidity, a lost passage of natural purity.

I smiled in wonder. I wished I were on foot, to savor every detail.

Then Greggan shifted gears and we began to climb. He was watching the slopes as he drove, as if looking for something, and suddenly he braked again and whispered, "See there!"

I ducked my head to scan the banks rising steeply around us but could see nothing.

"Two hinds and a stag!" he breathed.

I saw the shapes just before they vanished — faraway phantoms bounding weightlessly over a crest. Nothing was as near as my eye judged it to be.

He drove on. "They should be culled, you know." He was advising me as a landowner, but there was a familiar note of reproach in his voice. "There are too many hinds."

"The cull starts soon, doesn't it?"

"We start tomorrow."

"If — if I were to give you permission to cull the deer on my land —?"

He glanced out the window at his side before answering, as though quelling his first impulsive words. He assumed a set dry expression. "It takes all the hands I can muster to cull the herds on my own land," he told me. Then the blue eyes sent me a glint of amusement. "Are you fully aware, Mrs. MacLarkie, of the extent of your holdings?"

I took up the map and the accompanying page of itemized statistics, which I'd barely glanced at in the castle, and read them over. "Good heavens, it's nearly four thousand acres! Can that be right?"

"It is right," he said, with finality, and resumed his silence.

I was about to protest my innocence once more, but held my tongue. If he was entitled to his own complexities, he was entitled to his resentment.

But I felt our silence was not now the stiff isolating one we'd started out with; there seemed more communication between us even if we were at cross-purposes. And whether we were merely practicing restraint or had actually begun to develop mutual respect, it didn't matter, for it was more or less the same thing.

The hills were opening and we were climbing into high moorland. "See the brae yonder," he said, indicating the rise at the back of the moor. "You can view much of your land from there. I'll drive you as close as I can, and then, if you can manage, we'll walk the last bit."

"I can manage almost anything with my cane."

A faint flush came and went in his cheeks but I couldn't tell whether he was pleased or discomfited. "Hang on," he said, and the Land Rover turned off the track and went bucking and plunging over the rough terrain. I couldn't help laughing, clinging to a hand-grip over the door, and again he gave me a sharp speculative glance. We left the car at last and took to our legs through a slope of birch trees, and came out very soon on the grassy summit.

The land rolled off to the west and my eyes traveled over miles of moor and forest and vales, with a gleam of water here and there, to halt at last at a blue rampart of mountains.

I was still panting from the climb. "You'd better rest a moment," he said, and pulled off his plaid and made a rug of it for me. He seated himself on the grass a few feet away, clasping his forearms around his knees.

We were quiet a while, glorying in the view.

I might have said it was an empty place, except that as we sat there without speaking and my ear attuned itself to the minutiae of sound, I became aware of rustlings, sighings, faint twitterings, infinitesimal cracklings, and knew the place swarmed with secret life. The tranquillity settling over me wasn't mine to keep, or share, or believe in, but for these few moments I gave myself up to it. I didn't suppose I would ever come here again.

"I should think," I said finally, "your ancestors would have stood on this very vantage point. Does it have a name?"

A guttural jumble, which I took to be Gaelic, came from his lips. "It means Place of Peace. The heads of clans met here to arrange a truce or sort out a victory. Things were done in the open to avoid treachery. They were a fairly barbaric lot, even while the world to the south became more civilized."

We talked toward the scene below us, not looking at each other. "Is there a history one can read about them?" The record I'd read in the Kirkangus library had merely been a chronology of names and dates.

"About my ancestors? No. Their history has never been put together."

"What a pity."

"Aye, I agree. It's a saga of horrors and heroism and it oughtn't to go unrecorded." Clasping his knees, he lifted his heels and set them down again, and I sensed he was going to venture a little beyond the strictly impersonal. "In fact," he continued, "during the winter months when the castle is closed to guests, I occupy part of my time with assembling the history myself. I even have a publisher waiting for it in Edinburgh. Fortunately, he is a man of patience. It's painstaking work, and I'm a stickler for the truth."

I turned to him with a smile. As I'd suspected, the fish-catching, car-washing, rose-pruning man-of-all-work disguised more than a proud, stranded laird. Essentially he was a scholar, but even more than that a sensitive being, at the other end of the spectrum from the best marksman in the Highlands.

"It must demand laborious research," I murmured, to keep him talking.

"It does. It takes me far afield, to every sort of archive, from private libraries — some of them enchanting — to universities and government records. It's good for me. Otherwise, as Jean points out, I might become a sort of castle-mending machine." He brought an end to these personal recollections, breaking off to cry, "Look!" and pointing again. "It's the golden eagle!"

My eyes, not as keen as his, presently made out the soaring bird, wings motionless, high against the thin overcast. A little chill played across my shoulders. The solitary bird of prey crossing our field of vision seemed to me a reminder of hovering, inexorable cruelty. I shook myself. I was becoming omen-conscious.

"Susan," Greggan said, and at once I knew from his first use of my given name that he was about to take a plunge. Appointing himself my guide, bringing me to the Place of Peace, providing a handy rug to sit on, perhaps even letting down the bars about himself, all must have led up to this. "I think I'd better explain something to you."

III. . . .

I hesitated, almost preferring the inexplicable. "All right," I answered. "But please don't think you must explain anything for my sake."

"I must for mine. I don't go about as a rule behaving like a barbaric chieftain."

"I realize that, Lord Greggan." I couldn't bear his apologies. They were demeaning to us both. "I don't usually behave like a bitch in heat either."

He winced. "No. Even the words don't become you. Would you please call me Hugh?"

"I will call you Hugh." I had to hear him out. "You are the first Hugh I've ever known."

That gave him, I realize now, the perfect cue. "You are the first Susan I've known," he replied. "But not the first MacLarkie."

I stared, not sure what he meant. He was still facing the rolling sweep of land.

"This is what I must tell you," he said. "My

211

former wife was Gwendolyn MacLarkie."

My chest subsided over a long breath: I see, I see, I see ... His passion and fury, his bitterness and conscience, fell together now in a simple composition.

"I will add only this much," he continued, gazing grimly at the distant peaks, "but I owe it to you. It was not a happy marriage and it ended painfully. Gwendolyn eloped with a good-looking auto magnate from West Germany, who came up, originally, for the grouse ... and who can blame her?"

It was his tone of derision that gave me an inkling of his suffering. I thanked him. "No wonder a woman named MacLarkie is anathema to you. I thought it was due only to my husband's grandfather, who gobbled up so much of the Strathburne estate."

I saw his cheek crinkle slightly with a smile. "I wouldn't be straightforward," he told me, "if I didn't admit it added a wee bit to my prejudice." He turned to me at last. "But, Susan, you are not accountable for any of it. This is what causes me such remorse when I've vented my soreness on you. You merely married the name. While we're about it, what was your maiden name?"

"Burns." I grinned.

"I'm damned. You have Scots blood!" He was

smiling again. "This explains the hint of the mystic in you."

I was less sure of my new detachment now that he faced me. "Probably it explains the appeal of these hills."

"No, I mean a poetic quality. It lies in your face, even when you are half-drowned. Or when you're trying to size up your feelings in a chapel, not knowing anyone is looking at you."

My heart began to thump and my body irrepressibly, quite independently, threatened to melt again. Perhaps my eyes pleaded for a return to neutrality. His own chest rose and fell deeply and then he turned away again.

I said, to break the throbbing tension, "Do I look like Gwendolyn?" I wanted to know this.

"Not in the least, Gwendolyn has red hair," he replied shortly. When he spoke again his voice had quieted, shifting down to a slower tempo. "You are like smoke, Susan, like the gentle veil of the night. I picture you in the ruby-red dress of a crusader's lady, waiting in a tower." It was a verbal abandon greater then anything he'd permitted himself so far, yet he wasn't abashed by it, sitting with his face averted.

It took me a few seconds to find my voice. "Well, then, that's all right. I don't think you'll get us mixed up any more."

"I never did. I tried to and failed. I am simply on the defensive, I suppose, with a lovely woman."

I folded my hands tightly in my lap. We were on a new footing now but I didn't know what it was, hadn't the fortitude to think what it was.

"Do you mourn your husband still, Susan?"

Again I felt shaken, caught unaware. Did I mourn him still? I answered, thinking loud, "He doesn't belong to me in that way any more."

"A mystical reply if ever there was one. Well, but there is a shadow over you. If it's not sadness, then what is it? The child you lost? Or do you still suffer physical pain?"

"No." I studied the diminishing ranks of color before me, gold fading to bronze, lavender to blue, and listened to the stirrings of the air and the grass. In a sense he forced me to come to grips with truth, to leave off mysticism and face facts. But how could I tell him, *Someone is trying to kill me?* How could I tell him, I've come to mistrust everyone who has something to gain by my death — even you, Hugh Greggan. I couldn't even tell myself.

Again he turned to me. "I've no right to press you, but something does trouble you, doesn't it?"

"Hugh —" I began, and couldn't go on.

214

With a flash of blond knees he came to my side. I never thought to be afraid of him. He unclasped my hands, held them close to his chest. "Susan, can ye no' tell me?"

His nearness, his warm hands over mine, nearly overwhelmed me. "No," I gasped, short of breath. "I can't, Hugh. I can't. Don't worry. It will pass."

"I would take it away if I could, ye ken."

"Aye, Hugh." When he reverts in agitation to dialect I find myself responding in kind.

Releasing one hand, he kept the other, pressed it, held it to his cheek, kissed the back, and the palm, then released it, too. He turned away, clasped his knees again. He shut his eyes and said softly, "Susan, Susan . . ."

I had the sensation, listening to the tiny rustlings around us, of life standing still, of everything poised in precarious balance. One word, one motion, and our lives would change forever, irrevocably. I couldn't make this momentous transition, not now. I thought I knew what he wanted to say and I couldn't let him say it. I knew what I wanted to answer. I felt as if tears rained down silently within me.

"Hugh. Forgive me. We'd better go now."

He faced me. His eyes were the color of larkspur. "If that is your wish."

Every militant cell of my body urged me to

give way, quitting self-indulgent inner tears. How delicious, how unpretending and incorrupt, to fall back together, under the open milky sky, in the midst of this lonely, lively wilderness! My voice shook.

"It is not my wish, Hugh. But you've had enough heartache, due to the MacLarkies, and I have all the difficulty I can handle at the moment." Slowly I got to my feet.

He rose and followed without a word.

But at the car he halted me, resting a hand on my shoulder. "You will do me the favor," he said, "of letting me know if I can be of help to you."

I nodded. My hopelessness made it impossible to speak.

He still detained me. Both hands, now, clasped my shoulders. "You will do me the honor?"

Again I nodded. His eyes held mine sternly. He gave me a long level look, quite unreadable, a look perhaps of resignation, or release, or trust in what was unknown to him. Perhaps it was a pledge, and I was meant to accept it. Perhaps on the contrary his thoughts were quite different from what I imagined — alien and bitter once more. I sensed a tension running from his hands into my flesh. I braced myself. I was still not afraid.

But his hands fell away.

He opened the car door for me and I got in, and we set out for home, once more, as we had begun, in silence.

CHAPTER 12

I. . . .

The *ceilidh* was in full swing as we approached
the building. Thumping and clapping throbbed
in the night air. There were five of us – Jean
and I, Colin and Gordon, and as a last minute
replacement for Lilah, the lad, speechless with
joy at being included.

"No," Lilah insisted at dinner, despite Colin's
coaxing, "I'm not going. That kind of carousal
makes me nervous. I'd spoil your fun. I'm going
to play Scrabble with Wilbur Grant, and then
get to bed early."

There was no way I could lock my door and
leave my room safe from someone else's key. In
the end, feeling foolish again, I left a black
thread in the doorjamb, close to the floor.

In the hall downstairs Lilah put her cheek to
mine. "Enjoy yourself, dear. Forget everything
and have a good time!" As if in conditioned
reflex the old tenderness tried to awaken in me.
I caught Colin's eye over her shoulder: did he

218

read my feelings? I wondered what Lilah meant by *Forget everything*.

But once we were squeezed into Jean's little English Ford I did pretty much forget everything. I made up my mind to. A school's-out mood possessed us. The nonsense commenced immediately over Severn's liberal use of aftershave lotion — raillery which did nothing to diminish his joy. Gordon showed a polished Old World aptitude for revelry, while Jean in her offhand way kept him in check or spurred him on, and Colin was more than equal to them both.

My former energy and bubbling inner laughter returned. Something about the afternoon with Hugh Greggan had restored a sense of my right to existence, a faith in my own reality rather than an inevitable, unknown, external fate.

It may have come about from the truce we had made at the Place of Peace. Or perhaps it was simply that I'd accomplished what I'd come to Scotland to do. Whatever the cause, I was happier tonight than I'd been in a very long time.

The *ceilidh* was held in an old schoolhouse, a stone building no longer large enough to contain the schoolchildren of Kirkangus, let alone a regional gathering of elders. They spilled out

219

into the dark around the door. We entered to a general turbulence of noise, heat, and motion, pushed our way through a motley stag line, and joined the whirling throng.

Colin turned to me. "We'll go slowly," he promised. "Don't be afraid. I'll hold you." A fiddler, a drummer, and a red-faced lady-pianist provided music from the stage at the end of the room, and I found myself gliding sedately but in perfect slow-time around the floor.

The stout postmistress was there, the gentle hairdresser. Mr. Archibald MacBaine danced with a plump, rosy-faced woman who must surely be Mrs. Archibald. Along the wall in a row of dignitaries sat the Reverend Thornhill in animated conversation with a priest, his great baritone carrying even over the music. On his other side sat a handsome gray-haired woman with the strong patient face of one who has mastered life with an obstreperous husband, and when Jean and Gordon stopped to greet her fondly I knew this must be Mrs. Thornhill.

"You are lit up like a Christmas tree," said Colin in my ear. "Are you in love?"

"Yes," I told him. "I'm in love with being alive."

"Ah now, that's what I like to hear." His cheek rested lightly against my temple. He is a good dancer and his firm grasp never allowed me to lose my balance. "I was afraid you might be losing your heart to the lusty laird."

My pulse gave an odd little bounce, but I answered, "That would be the height of madness, wouldn't it?"

"Maybe not the height, but partway up. I'd hate for you to bury yourself here in the back of beyond, now that you're really alive."

"Maybe I'm not cut out for the California country-club life."

"You're not. You were cut out for something much more romantic. A palazzo in Venice. A casbah in Marrakesh. A houseboat in Kashmir . . ."

"That's what you're cut out for, Colin. I need to put down roots. And speaking of romance, how would you like to play Cupid?"

He drew back, missing a beat. "For you, Susan?" He rarely called me Susan. "You're serious then — about the laird?"

"I'm not serious about anything now, except living. No, for Jean. She and Gordon were made for each other, in my humble opinion, but they don't know it. Without creating too much havoc, would you like to give her a rush and try rousing Gordon's jealousy?"

Colin laughed. "You *are* a sly one! Aren't you really asking me to divert Gordon from a heartbreaking infatuation with you?"

"Gordon's heart doesn't break that easily."

"In your humble opinion. All right, I'll try it! I'd enjoy playing Cupid in a Highland romance. When do I start?"

"Now."

We intercepted Gordon and Jean, dancing with practiced ease.

"Shall we change partners?" said Colin. "You're dying to dance with Susan, Jocko, and I'm dying to dance with this flower of Scotland." He took Jean in his arms. "Do you trust yourself with a California sex fiend?"

She sparkled. "Only in a crowd, laddie boy."

"But you have no idea how pleasing I can be alone. Let me tell you about it. Ta, Sue-love! See you later, laddie boy." And Colin, ogling Jean at close range, whirled her away.

"Cheeky fellow!" Absentmindedly Gordon embraced me, his eyes following Colin. "What's come over him? I didn't think he had leanings in that direction." We began to dance. "Is he really such a woman-chaser?"

"Oh yes." I shook my head as if over unfortunate experience. "I'm afraid he's been building up a thing for Jean. Can she take care of herself all right?"

"Of course she can," he snapped irritably, as if at Jean herself. He drew me closer. "In any case, he's played into my hands. Here I am at last, holding you as I've longed to!"

"You'll have to go more slowly, Gordon. I can't keep up this mad pace."

"Oh my God, forgive me, I got carried away. I've never been this near to you. You *are* much better, aren't you? You won't always be —" He hesitated.

"Lame?" I gave him a brave smile. "I *hope* not!" But I didn't sound confident.

"Alas, you'd better not try the reels tonight."

"The reels? When do they start?"

"As soon as everyone's properly warmed up. The bottle must pass a few more times outside in the dark. Look, if Jean can dance with a sex fiend, you can try a reel with me. I'll see to it your feet never touch the floor."

This picture broke up my brave, pathetic expression, and Gordon at once went into his trancelike stare. "Oh, Susan . . . !"

"It's you and Jean I want to watch dancing the reel, Gordon. You make a dazzling pair."

"Do we?" He sighed, emerging from his trance. For the first time I thought he overdid it a bit. "She *is* a dear, isn't she?"

"Colin would spirit her away to Hollywood if he could. Don't let him hold her in his arms too long, he's really very persuasive. I wouldn't want him to take her outside in the dark."

"He'd better not!" Like an RAF pilot scanning the horizon in an old movie, Gordon cast an eye over the bobbing heads. "Have no fear, I'll attend to him."

"Gordon, I'm a little tired. I think I'll sit on the sidelines for a little while."

"Are you sure?" he asked anxiously. He was dying to go to Jean's rescue and he felt guilty about it. "Will you be all right?"

He led me over to the benches against the wall, introduced me to his mother, and with a handsome Battle-of-Britain expression set out at once on his mission. I had to smile at myself, that I could be a little taken aback at his giving me up so willingly.

His mother patted the space beside her and I sat down and we entered into friendly talk, interrupted now and then by vocalizations from her husband. The music halted at last and Colin joined us, bringing me a sweet orange drink and surreptitiously giving me a thumb-and-forefinger circle. Gordon and Jean in a far corner appeared to be having a heated discussion.

Everyone milled about for a while, and tension mounted. Severn could be seen in *dégagé* conversation with a bosomy young woman in electric blue. He was puffing on a cigarette, his eyes watering.

At last the musicians filed back on the stage,

a roar went up, and the dancers began to form in eights.

"You'll excuse us, Mrs. MacLarkie?" Mr. Thornhill drew his wife to her feet. "We make up in pluck what we lack in stamina, withal!"

"Foolhardiness," Mrs. Thornhill amended calmly, "rather than pluck, is what we have in abundance." They took their places.

With a roll of the drum and a shout the reel began. It was bedlam. Shrieks and yells arose. I clapped in unison with the bystanders.

Jean was a delight to watch, hands poised, shoulders level, alert and graceful, and the nimble Gordon was in his element. Even Colin joined the fray, commandeered by Jean, who when he made a wrong turn laughingly seized him and shoved him in the right direction. It seemed almost as if she were playing our game. Gordon shot daggers out of the corners of his eyes.

Mrs. Thornhill tripped to the beat in a skilled, conservative way, but Mr. Thornhill sprang about, knees high, like a schooled horse. In a distant circle bobbed the shining face of Archibald MacBaine.

But it was Severn who held my eyes. Buoyant as a feather, proud in bearing, fair of face, he danced in the old-fashioned way, with dignity, like a young prince disporting.

Of course, it would have been all the more stirring if the dancers had worn native dress. They were clothed in everything from black Sunday-best to blue jeans, and there wasn't a kilt in sight.

Colin longs to wear one, but sooner in California than Scotland, he says. In Scotland taking liberties with tartans, as tourists blithely do, or wearing Tam O' Shanters for comic effect, gives rise to private ridicule, if not affront, and may have contributed to the dying out of the costume.

So the uniqueness of Hugh Greggan struck me all the more forcibly, and his individualism seemed to me all the more admirable. My thoughts were never free of him for long. I wished he could have been present. I was sure he could dance the reel, too, or had danced it when he was young and lighthearted, and I pictured him, stately as Severn, graceful as Jean, nimble as Gordon.

He was getting his sleep, Jean had told us, before rising at dawn for the hind cull.

II. . . .

It was nearly one o'clock when we returned to the castle. Moonlight, opaque behind the clouds, gave a strange pallor to the loch.

Colin touched my arm as we rounded the

bend to the causeway. "Let's get out and walk the rest of the way. My head needs clearing."

"You'll have had your fill of uproarious Scots," said Gordon, stopping the car squarely on the bridge. His aplomb was by this time stretched to the limit. "A pleasant good night to you." And with a flurry of gravel he drove off, while Jean and Severn, taken unawares, looked back and waved.

Openmouthed, Colin and I watched the tail-lights vanish. Then we turned to each other and doubled over with laughter.

"Disgruntled, wouldn't you say, is the word for our Jocko?"

"He'll pack Severn off to bed," I said, "and then he and Jean will have an unholy row, followed by a touching scene of reconciliation, and after that, if we've done our job, an exchange of vows."

"You may be right. There's wizardry in you, Susan." He turned to the view of the dark castle jutting out over the water. "That's what I wanted to see: the castle by moonlight." He leaned on the stone parapet. "Doesn't it remind you of a Victorian engraving?" I forget sometimes that he is an artist. "One of those lurid landscapes with bats flying about and a couple of terrified people showing the whites of their eyes?"

The mass of stonework towered black against the mottled, moon-clouded sky. Only one or two lights shone out, probably nightlights in the halls. The air was cold and faintly sour, smelling of the pale sleeping lake and dying foliage. "It's a stage set for *Macbeth*," I whispered.

"Okay, no more gloomy talk." He took my arm. "We mustn't end a super evening on this note. You did enjoy yourself, didn't you?"

"Oh, yes! You're good for me, Colin. I'd never have gone to the *ceilidh* at all if you hadn't insisted."

"Did I make you forget everything?"

I didn't understand. "What — ?"

"As Lilah advised."

"Oh, of course. I'd forgotten she said it!" We laughed again, leaning over the water below. *There is a shadow over you*, Hugh had said. It was true, for a little while tonight I'd been free of it, and I'd let down my guard completely.

Colin said, "We'd better do something about Lilah, don't you think?"

"About Lilah? Why do you say that?"

"She's so quiet, so docile. Ever since Dottie went to the hospital she's been such an angel. When Lilah is on her best behavior I can't help wondering what's going on in her head, what she's building up to. I've

228

seen her like this before."

I drew a little away from him. "What are you trying to say, Colin?" Was he warning me, too?

"I never *try* to say anything, sweetheart. If I can say it at all, I say it." He turned me about. "Come on, let's go in. I didn't mean to alarm you. I merely think she bears watching. Maybe she just needs a little special attention, a little buttering up. She'll know we had a good time tonight and she'll feel left out, even though we begged her to come. Maybe I'd better cook up some amusement for her."

I held back. "What did you mean, you've seen her like this before?" I couldn't help myself. I had to stop trying to say what I wanted to say and, like Colin, say it. "Was it — was that — before Bart died?"

His arm in mine gently drew me forward, and we moved off the bridge. "No, I didn't see much of Lilah, or anyone else in the family, before Bart died. I was busy on special effects for 'Cops.' "

In the in-group fashion he abbreviated titles, and I surprised myself by remembering the full name of the series he referred to: "Cops, Robbers, and Fallen Angels." It was as if bits and pieces of my amnesia for the time preceding Bart's death were breaking off and falling away, like the earth from an archaeologist's find;

perhaps someday the whole article would be revealed.

Colin continued: "No, it was some time before Bart died, before you even knew him." He was silent a fraction of a second as if making up his mind. "It was before Andrew died."

I stood perfectly still at the bottom of the bridge. "You're serious now, aren't you?" Perhaps I didn't quite trust Colin either. "You're not playing games?"

"Sue-love," he said, peering at me in the glimmering half-dark, the moonlight gleaming on his hair, making sockets of his eyes, "don't you know how it is with clowns?" His boyish face wasn't smiling, his eyes weren't laughing. "Underneath we are always serious."

"Yes. All right. I believe you." I didn't want to hear any more. I didn't want to know what Colin suspected, if he suspected anything. Dottie's suspicions were bad enough. If I'd asked Colin to explain what he meant about Lilah and Andrew, he probably would have done so, but he must have known from my face that I didn't want him to.

We approached the ramp. "Let's talk about the *ceilidh*," he said. "I always think comparing notes after a party is half the —"

But I had halted in my tracks once more, clutching his arm.

"My God, Sue, what is it?"

We were almost under the castle wall and I had looked up. A ghostly figure stood in a window over us, a window in our upstairs hall. But the moment I looked up it vanished with a flutter of garments. Surely Lady Fanquill wasn't on the prowl at this time of night?

I stood holding my breath a moment longer. "Nothing, Colin. I must be seeing ghosts."

"It's the moonlight, darling. It creates all sorts of illusions. Come on, it's time you were in bed!"

He saw me to my room. I didn't want him to know the extent of my fears or the lengths I was going to, to protect myself, so I couldn't bring myself to squat down and see if the black thread had been dislodged.

"Sweet dreams!" he whispered, and kissed me lightly on the cheek.

I went in and locked my doors.

I went through the routine of checking my room, even looking under my bed. I keep my journal locked in my dressing case, which in turn is locked in a desk drawer, and I could find no scratch marks on the locks. Everything appeared to be as I left it.

Afterward, I lay awake, thinking about Andrew MacLarkie — a strapping fellow, evidently, with a weak business head. He'd had a history of heart trouble, there was no question about that; but now I knew that Colin as well as Dottie wondered about Andrew's final attack.

God, I entreated, am I going mad?

I couldn't go on this way — leaving threads in the door, rinsing carafes, alternately seeing ghosts and hiding my head in the sand. I couldn't pack up and run, leaving Dottie in the hospital. There was nowhere to run, anyway, where I couldn't be followed. And it was not one person alone I'd have to run from but several, for now I shrank from everyone.

I was not safe anywhere.

CHAPTER 13

I. . . .

I awoke very early to the sound of distant rifle fire. Two explosive cracks ripped in rapid succession through the silence of the hills, ricocheted back and forth over the glens, and melted finally into the all-absorbing stillness of dawn.

The stalking season had begun.

A working design of sinew, flesh, and bone, with at its heart the super-spark — *life* — was at this moment passing into extinction. I burrowed my head into my pillows and covered my ears. Hugh Greggan himself might have fired those shots. He never missed.

I could picture him clasping his knees, his weather-tanned face in profile, the old Strathburne acres flooding away beyond him, and I could remember how I felt beside him in that wilderness, how tranquillity had settled on me even though I knew tranquillity wasn't mine to keep.

233

Perhaps the truth was, when one learned to love life one accepted all of it, the brutal and the benign.

I slept again.

It was after ten when I awoke for the second time. Chrissie brought me a note with my breakfast.

Sue-love: Am driving over to Inverness to do some shopping. Dougal is going to take me deer stalking tomorrow and I must get some boots. (Can you believe, I once won a sharpshooter's medal. Bart, of course, won three!) Invited Lilah to go with me and she's tickled pink. Probably won't be back till after tea. Have a loverly day. XXXOOO Colin.

He was as good as his word. He may have cooked up the whole thing to amuse Lilah. I could breathe freely for a few hours. After breakfast I attended to my business mail and caught up on my journal, and didn't leave my room until noon.

I stopped at the desk to post my letters. "No ill effects from our athletics last night?" asked Jean with a grin. But she looked for once a trifle hollow-eyed.

"I slept it off. I wish you could have, too."

"Och, I shall tonight. It was worth it."

And she gave me a sort of crinkled smile with a warm humorous look that said in the space of

a second that her world had taken a revolution-
ary turn for the better which she hadn't quite
adjusted to yet, that she suspected I had a little
something to do with it, and that she hoped my
world would turn out as well. I gave her a
crinkled smile in return which said, Yes, I hope
so too, and I'm glad for you and thank you for
confiding in me.

The dining room has thinned out this week.
Only the Barsington-Bankses, Wilbur Grant,
and Lady Fanquill are left in the castle, besides
the MacLarkies. We are the diehards. In another week the castle will close.

Lady Fanquill beckoned to me from her table,
and at her invitation I sat down to lunch with
her.

Gordon, attending us, was hollow-eyed also,
and slightly stunned, but he was the same
irrepressible Jocko. Over Lady Fanquill's head
he gave me a smile, not crinkled but impudent,
as if to say, I may have discovered the darling of
my life but I will always have eyes for a
beautiful woman.

Jean with her crisp light touch will manage
him if anyone can. And I thought, as I'd
thought of Jean, Surely I have nothing to fear
from Gordon Thornhill!

Lady Fanquill and I exchanged small talk for
a while. She told me she would be returning to

235

her house in Edinburgh soon. I steered her into telling me about herself, about growing up in this very castle. It was a childhood of bleak discomfort, which she's never regretted. "It toughened me," she said, delicately buttering a roll with almost transparent hands, "and it served me well as a civil servant's wife in some rather cheerless outposts."

Then with scarcely a pause she continued, "One was made to fit a mold in those days, and one did not complain. But it was harder on my nephew." And she went on to describe Hugh Greggan's upbringing, and a picture unfolded of an only child who loved nature and was happiest in his native Highlands but who was sent away to spartan boarding schools and on to military training at Sandhurst. "His face," said his aunt, "has never lost the stamp of loneliness."

Now I knew when the haunted expression had begun, where he'd acquired his stoicism, how the hawk and the dove had come to be caged within him. My heart ached for the boy he once was.

"Yes," said Lady Fanquill, perhaps readings the expression in my eyes, "but sometimes the survivors of such severity become heroes." She considered a moment, and re-marked with her oblique logic, "It is a wonder he does not stammer."

"At least," I said, "he has his Highlands again, his golden eagle. He has Jean."

"Indeed," Lady Fanquill replied, lifting her head proudly. "And he has never been one to feel sorry for himself."

She wished me to understand him, but not to pity him.

We had finished our lunch and I said I must leave for Kirkangus. But Lady Fanquill detained me, searching in her handbag — a soft tasseled sack made of russet velvet. "I found a talisman for you," she said, handing me a little packet of tissue paper. "It was given me by my grandmother. Open it when you are alone and wear it."

I stopped the car on the bridge and unwrapped the tissue paper. It contained a tiny thistle of old gold, its blossom carved out of amethyst. I held it for a moment, looking out over the loch, my heart full and heavy. I must part with a number of people I'd come to love. I thought, There isn't much time left.

I pinned the thistle on my lapel and drove on.

II. . . .

"He's got a will of iron, that little Scotchman!" Dottie flopped around on her bed, wagging her head like a captive seal. It amused me that big

Dottie O. had met her match in small Dr. Craigie. "He says I'm okay to go home tomorrow but not before. Jesus, kiddo, will you talk to him?"

"Ha ha, Mrs. O'Halloran. Yes. I'll ask him to outline some exercises and appoint me to stand over you while you do them. Dottie, he's right. This is the first day you've sat up."

"Yeah, and while I sit, time may be running out on you!"

"It may be." I got up to stand in the window. "I've almost reached the point where I'd rather have it run out than go on with this waiting. I'm tempted to tell everyone you're coming home tomorrow and bring on a showdown."

"Oh no. No." She rolled her head on the pillow. "Sue, you mustn't. Stick it out one more day. Sue, promise me." She struggled to rise. "Promise me you won't tell them or I will leave now against medical advice!"

I flew to her bed and restrained her. "Yes, all right, I promise! Lie down, Dottie!"

She fell back, her face pale and damp. We both knew then that Dr. Craigie was right to keep her another day. She said weakly, "Sue, we're due to leave Monday for the States, right? Supposing, after I get out of here, supposing you tell Lilah you've decided to stay on awhile. She'd have no choice but to go home without you. And I'll stay on with you until she goes."

Lilah. Dottie always came back to Lilah. And it was Lilah who had said, Don't let Dottie become a fixture in your life.

"We can't stay on, Dottie. The hotel closes Monday for the winter."

She deliberated. "All right, you could do some more traveling on your own. I could stay with you long enough for you to get started."

Lilah had said, She doesn't want you to trust me. I looked at Dottie. It didn't seem to matter any more whether I trusted or didn't trust. I said, "I can't run from Lilah the rest of my life." I wasn't even sure it was Lilah I should be running from.

I moved to the end of Dottie's bed and gripped the footrail. "Dottie, I want you to know this. Maybe it will reassure you. When you said *One murder is enough* it turned something to iron in me, some part of me that had always been weak and confused. It wasn't one murder, Dottie, if murder was done: my baby was killed, too. My pregnancy constituted another heir. Neat, wasn't it, killing two birds with one stone — three, they hoped? Dottie, whether it was murder or a true accident, that iron in me has changed the situation, and I'm not as helpless as I was a week ago, and maybe I don't need a protector or someone to lean on." I grinned. "How do you like them apples? You wanted me to stand on my own two feet, right? Well, at last I think I am about to do that." I headed for the door, then turned. "And incidentally, last night I went dancing."

"You — *what*?"

"Yeah. Ha ha, Mrs. O'Halloran. Behave yourself, and I'll come for you tomorrow."

She was still openmouthed as I saluted and went out the door.

III. . . .

My next call was upon Mr. Archibald Mac-Baine, who all agleam came tripping across his office to greet me. Again he settled me face to face with him as if for a celebration, hands at the ready on his knees, tidy feet poised to leap or bound or skip.

We exchanged compliments on our dexterity and hardihood at the *ceilidh*, and then I stated my business.

The amiable gleam never left his face but his plump tweed-clad body went perfectly still. "What, all of it, Mrs. MacLarkie?"

"All of it, Mr. MacBaine. What good is it to me? And why should Lord Greggan have to wait for it until I die? You will have to figure out how it can be done, and I'd rather Lord Greggan didn't know about

240

it until after I leave Monday."

Mr. MacBaine's gold-rimmed eyes were bright but steady. Softly he said, "I will respect your wishes, my lady."

"I'm sure there'll be lots of papers to sign. If you can have them ready for me before I leave I'll come in and sign them."

"I will do whatever is possible, and notify you."

I moved to rise and he clapped his hands to his knees and leaped to his feet. He put out his plump little hand and I put mine in it. "Mrs. MacLarkie," he said, "you do honor to your husband's name."

If it had been within the bounds of Scottish law-office propriety I'd have given him a hug. As it was, we nodded and twinkled, and then he trotted me to the door and down the stairs and all the way out to the street.

IV. . . .

Mrs. Kenzie's cat was seated on the porch where I'd last seen him, and as I came up the walk he half-rose on his haunches and opened his mouth soundlessly in greeting. He would accompany me inside, he told me in body language, curling his tail persuasively about my ankles. I rang the bell.

"Och, ye've come!" cried Mrs. Kenzie, with a

241

broad smile, and drew me indoors. She produced a tea tray in short order and we settled ourselves in our former places in the parlor. A coal fire burned in the grate against the chill of the October day. The cat seated himself contentedly between us and indulged in open-eyed reverie.

"Ye didn't hold it against me then, that I sent you away so disappointed!" Mrs. Kenzie handed me a pretty cup decorated with violets and the statement in gold script, *A Cup o' Kindness from Aberdeen*. "I couldn't forget the look on your face!"

"Of course I don't hold it against you, Mrs. MacLarkie —"

"Ye may call me Margaret if ye like."

"Thank you, Margaret." But if ever there was a Peggy, especially in her youth, this petite redhead was one. "And you must call me Susan. No, I'm sure in your place I'd have felt unjustly put on the spot."

"Aye, but the fact is, I'm not a bad judge of character, and I knew ye had nought but kindness in your heart." She pointed to the large tinted photograph over the mantel. "It was that portrait there of my good husband Kenzie, and those eyes reproaching me, that told me I'd been less than kind myself."

"You were only trying to protect his good

name!" I glanced respectfully at Kenzie's stern, moustached countenance. "Anyway, Margaret, I've learned since I saw you that the Earl of Strathburne's unhappy marriage was to a Gwendolyn MacLarkie. Was she from your husband's branch of the family — or mine?"

Margaret's eyes turned to the glowing coals. They had filled with the same anguish I'd seen in her eyes on my first visit, and much the same as the anguish I'd seen in the eyes of Hugh Greggan.

"She was our child," said Margaret Mac-Larkie in a whisper.

The ginger cat turned its meditative gaze upon her. I sat perfectly still leaning forward over my cup.

"She came from your husband's branch of the family. She ran away from her brother when she was nine, and Kenzie and I, being childless, took her in. She was an orphan, and we went to the law and adopted her."

Margaret set down her cup.

"Och, if you could have seen her when she came to us! Well, she was dirty, that's all, from her tangled hair to her poor wee bare feet. But beneath the filth she was a beauty. And she took to cleanliness, she loved pretty things, she was quick to learn the social airs and graces." Margaret turned to me. "Because she had a canny head on her shoulders. All the MacLarkies are canny! By the time she was seventeen she was teaching the singing classes in the same Kirkangus school where I had taught myself!"

So I had guessed correctly about Margaret.

Her voice, which a few moments before had nearly broken, was firmer. "She was the prettiest girl for miles around. The lads flocked about her, but she was canny enough to keep her reputation spotless, and in the end she spurned them all. The life of a farmer's wife was not for her. I would not be surprised, Susan, if she had her bonnet set for the young laird all along."

I let her refill my cup.

She seemed to debate whether to continue, and then did so, but the anguish never left her eyes. "Aye, well, she had a cool head and she was pretty, but the heart got left out. She didn't have a soul, she didn't have a conscience. Perhaps her wretched beginnings told on her; perhaps it was in her blood. Accomplished though she was, on the outside, she was as wild as mountain heather within."

I murmured, "I can almost guess what happened. She sang in the kirk of Kirkangus. The laird saw her every Sunday. The laird fell in love with her."

Margaret nodded. "Just so. They slipped

away and were married without ceremony. The laird's kin were opposed to the match, and many said he married beneath him, although she was as near a lady as she could be, more of a lady than I myself who taught her all I knew." The bright eyes lifted to me. "But I could not teach her charity!"

"Margaret, the Earl may have fallen in love with that very wildness in her."

She studied me. "You may be right. He loved his wild Highlands, and with her fiery hair she was like a mountain spirit from the old legends. But it wasn't a wildness one could live at peace with."

She hesitated again, and I waited. The ginger cat, unmoved by the intensity of our talk, folded himself on the hearth rug, tucking one front paw and then the other under the pillow of his chest, and sealing his lids.

"I only pray," said Margaret at last, "that Gwendolyn gave him some measure of happiness in the beginning. He'd been a brave lonely youth, a soldier trained against his nature, and he needed tenderness. She may have enjoyed being Countess for a while, and lady of the manor. But it didn't stand for much when they were so hard up, and they had to take in paying guests, and after Jean was born she was filled with discontent. I saw little of her but I heard the rumors. She was not careful of her reputation any more. Jean was brought up by nurses and the laird himself. So the marriage had turned to ashes long before the foreigner came from Germany with his show of wealth, and even though the divorce was a public disgrace, ye might say it was a deliverance for them both."

A little glass-domed clock ticked beneath Kenzie's portrait.

"Is she happier, do you think," I asked, "with the auto magnate?"

"Och, she's not married to *him* any more! To tell the truth, Susan, I don't know whom she's with now. She lives in style in the south of France when she's not a-wandering. She'll never be tamed! I haven't seen her in years but I pray for that lost soul of hers, night and day!"

"Ah, Margaret, how tragic for you."

"Nay, it was Kenzie whose heart was broken. He loved that child!" Now at least tears welled in her eyes, and she rummaged for a handkerchief in the pocket of her cardigan and quickly dabbed the tears away. "But, you see, he loved her with all her faults, and I loved her in spite of them, and there's the difference." She put away her handkerchief and smiled at me. "Now, lass, I've talked heart-to-heart with you as I haven't done with anyone else."

I understood. She had concerned herself for

me and opened her heart to me because my youth, my widowhood, and my crutch had touched the same soft spot the orphaned Gwendolyn had touched.

"You said she ran away from her brother. Was that Murdo MacLarkie?"

She shuddered. "Aye, it was!"

"Well, no wonder she had a wild streak. I went to see him after I called on you."

"Och, I was afraid ye might do that! He dinna lay a hand on you, did he?"

"No, but I had to run for it."

She shook her head. "He's lucky he's never been certified and sent away. God must have blinded him as a vengeance."

"And to give blunderers like me a sporting chance." Robert Barton MacLarkie had handed down a tendency to lechery, it seemed, tempered to virility in the American strain. "Well, I thank you, Margaret, for clearing it all up for me. I know it wasn't easy for you. I mustn't take up any more of your —"

"Stay, lass. It isn't often I have a chance to visit with a young woman, one I can be so at ease with. Jean comes frequently in winter, but from spring to autumn the castle takes up most of her time."

So Margaret made a fresh pot of tea and heated some scones, and we sat by her warm

247

fire for another hour. I told her about Bart and his brothers, and she told me about her years of teaching in Kirkangus, in the same stone building where I'd danced last night, and we compared notes on Scotland and the United States, and when we finally parted I bent down and we put our arms around each other.

"I count you as a friend, Margaret. We'll write to each other, shall we?"

If I live, the inner voice spoke up again, and I suddenly felt cold.

Margaret waved me off cheerfully, and this time the ginger cat escorted me all the way to the gate.

But there he lost interest in me. Putting his nose out to the street he took stock of the savage world of Kirkangus; his eyes widened, his pupils dilated, and he commenced ferociously to lash his tail.

CHAPTER 14

I. . . .

Daylight was already fading and a fine rain fell.
Again the long moor seemed ominously still
and gray, and the drop to the loch through the
dripping firs was like descending into a
netherworld which grew more menacing and
inescapable with every turn.

The loch came into view and then the castle.
A few lights had already been turned on and
their reflections glinted down the breadth of the
dark water. I reached the garage gratefully and
berthed the car in its stall.

Colin's car was in the stall next to mine; he
and Lilah were home from Inverness ahead of
me. I'd hoped to miss them, getting to my room
via the back stairs and staying there until dinner
time, but I'd overstayed my time with Margaret
MacLarkie. I sat still for a moment, wearily
gathering up courage and caution once more.

Meanwhile the rain had begun pelting down,
running rivers over the cobblestones. I got out

of the car and hesitated under the shelter of the garage roof. If I walked to the door of the back stairs, halfway down the drive, I'd be soaked. I decided I'd better get back in the car, drive it around to the main entrance, and leave it for Munro to put away.

It was then I felt the first intimation of danger. It was as if someone breathed on the back of my neck. I felt the short hairs rise and then the longer ones, all the way to the top of my scalp. I could not go back to my car. I knew I must get out of the garage at once.

I ducked my head and ran for the archway into the stable and on directly to the door Severn had conducted me to, when I came to thank Hugh Greggan for rescuing me from the loch. I acted without thinking. I simply leaped forward as if catapulted. It was the nearest door I knew of, one that someone hiding in the garage might not know of, and I hoped I could lose whoever it was before they knew where I'd gone.

It was almost dark inside the little entry to the castle, and for half a second after I'd pushed the door shut I stood still, panting. I could hear nothing but the rush of rain outside. There was an ancient iron contrivance for a latch and after fumbling with it I gave up trying to lock the door. I felt I must hurry, and I set off quickly for the hall that ran alongside the kitchen, where the staff at this moment were no doubt making a cheerful racket preparing dinner.

I stopped short. Did I turn right or left? Right, I decided. I remembered Severn and I had followed the curve of the outer wall circling the moat. The dim light from an archer's slit high in the wall scarcely reached the lower part of the passage, so I transferred my cane to my left hand and put my right hand on the wall to guide myself. I was just in time to keep from falling down a flight of steps.

Was there a flight of steps before, with Severn? I hung back at the top, trying to remember. By now I doubted the wisdom of entering this maze at all. Perhaps I should turn and go back; perhaps my imagination had once again run away with me. Perhaps my suspicions, Dottie's, Lilah's, even Colin's, were all imaginary.

But the archer's slit indicated I was on the right track, skirting the moat, and I thought I might as well go on a little farther rather than turn back into the rain. I descended the steps into pitch darkness. I came to another stop.

And now I heard the footsteps.

They came from behind me, quick and light, and they halted a fraction of a second after mine did. My skin shriveled. Why would someone halt, and wait, and listen in silence, unless they were stalking me?

I opened my mouth to call out but held the sound back in my throat. My shoulders pushed against the stone as one pushes the floorboards of a car when someone drives dangerously. For a full minute there wasn't a sound except the heavy pumping of my own heart.

Perhaps I'd been mistaken? Perhaps the footfalls had been echoes of my own?

Then I heard it: the soft stealthy movement of a single step, carefully placed, and tentatively, one more.

Openmouthed, my own breath drying my throat, I clung to the wall in the darkness. Silently I took my cane across my waist in both hands, as I had done when Murdo MacLarkie advanced on me.

Another step, and another. They grew fainter. They were going away from me! They had taken the turn to the left.

I turned and ran on tiptoe, as silently and cautiously as possible. My eyes were adjusting to the darkness, but again I caught myself before plunging down another flight of stone steps.

I had no recollection of these two flights of steps on my previous trip with Severn, and I knew at last that somewhere I'd taken the wrong turn.

I couldn't go back now but I recognized the danger of going forward, heading downward. As I hovered at the top of the steps I thought I heard footsteps again. Was more than one person following? I took the steps two at a time, and even in my terror I was amazed at my agility.

The passage curved to the left and I felt a draft of cold air. A way out! A faint light revealed a shorter set of steps and another curve in the wall, and now I was running without touching my cane to the ground, without even trying to muffle my footfalls, my only thought to reach the safe out-of-doors and there, if necessary, face the stalker. The draft grew stronger and colder as I ran.

I rounded the curve and with an intake of breath like an inverted scream I hurled myself against the wall and slid to the stone floor. If there hadn't been a pale trace of daylight I might not have seen what was coming; or perhaps it was the faint sigh of moving water that warned me in time. I remembered Severn mentioning the open drops. My cane clattered on the stone and rolled into the opening, about six feet in diameter, and disappeared with a little gurgling plop. Alas, my beloved cane.

I had come upon the hole, as Severn described it, for dumping bodies into.

I was lying, gasping as if winded, in the wedge of the stone floor and wall, and now the footsteps were coming quickly and inexorably, and I crawled into the darkest corner and huddled there, on the far rim of the glimmering hole.

What a terrible place to die, I thought.

The footsteps stopped. A voice said softly, "Susan?"

The blood which seemed concentrated suffocatingly in the base of my throat gave way and I breathed again. I scrambled up, almost sobbing.

"Hugh!"

II. . . .

We met on the other side of the hole. He opened his arms, and without thinking of danger I went straight into them.

"What in God's name – ?" he began, holding me, half-rocking me like a child. There was only a foot behind me, between me and the hole. If he wished to kill me, push me back into the cold rushing water, if this was finally the end, I couldn't help myself, I could no longer run, or hope, or care.

My lungs constricted by his grip, my voice muffled against him, I made garbled noises about rain and the underground way to the kitchen, and getting lost.

"My God, you almost ended up in the loch again!" His arms held me almost as if he would crush me. "I wasn't sure it was you, I was in the stable and thought I saw you hurrying by, in fact it was your slight limp that identified you, but I couldn't imagine what you were up to and I was afraid for you —" He, too, was out of breath. One of his hands clasped the back of my head, stroked my hair.

"Hugh, was there someone else, someone following me?"

"Yes, I think so."

"Man or woman?"

"I couldn't tell in the dusk and rain. Whoever it was, they took the turn to the kitchen. I heard the footsteps going away. Susan, were you running from them? Did this person mean you harm?"

I wasn't afraid now. The same tranquillity, the same illusion of security I'd felt with him at the Place of Peace, lulled me now, made me almost indifferent. "I don't know, Hugh," I murmured. "I don't know."

"You still can't tell me, can you? You still can't tell me what it is that troubles you?"

I tried to pull away but his arms tightened. "Never mind," he said. "I'll not ask again.

You're cold. I must get you out of here. It will be black as night in no time." But still he held me.

"My cane, Hugh, my beautiful cane!" I cried suddenly. "It went down the hole!"

"It will come out in the loch. I'll find it for you."

His arms hadn't loosened their hold. His chest rose and fell more deeply. Then suddenly he let go, raised his hands to my face, tilting it upward, and kissed my forehead as if in a benediction, my eyelids, my cheekbones, and finally my lips, not opening them but pressing firmly, tellingly, and when this final kiss ended we both drew in a long uncertain breath.

"That is my message to you," said Hugh, his throat husky, "if you care to read it. And now take my hand."

At that moment in Hugh's arms, I realize afterward, I must finally have released Bart, stopped hammering at the gates of his silence. If I am to love being alive, I must live in the now and not yesterday, and leave the sleeping to their sleep. Bart himself would have wished it.

Hugh turned and led me back through the curving passages, up the flights of steps, then right, then left, and at last we were in the stable-yard entry.

My feet braked suddenly, I held back.

A figure moved there in the half-dark, whimpering like an animal in distress, wringing hand over hand.

"Lilah," I cried, not with surprise, but despair.

III. . . .

"Oh, Sue!" She flung out her arms and fell against me. "Oh, Sue!"

"Lilah, what —"

She gripped my wrists. She didn't seem aware of Hugh. The hood of her raincoat fell back as she raised her tear-streaked, rain-streaked face to me. "Oh, Susan, I've been looking for you. Are you all right? Oh, I'm so frightened —" Her teeth began to chatter.

"She's ill," said Hugh, putting an arm about her.

"Lilah, stop it!" If she was acting now, obliterating all suspicions, disarming me once more, she was succeeding; at least, it didn't seem to matter to me now, one way or the other. "Lilah, come. I'll help you to your room."

"I'll lead you through to the service hall," Hugh offered.

Lilah stumbled along with me, her sobs subsiding to a low burble. We came at last to the warm noisy corridor next to the kitchen and

Hugh stopped short of the door into the main hall.

"Would you like me to send for the doctor?"

"No," I told him, "I don't think it's necessary. I'll stay with her."

"Very well." He took my hand, clasped it within his. "Send for me if you need me." His kilt fanned out as he wheeled and left us. He was still in his heavy stalking boots.

Lilah, thoroughly disheveled, made an attempt to compose herself before going out into the main hall, and then, arm in arm, we proceeded through the door.

"Now then," I said, when I'd got her tucked into bed with a hot water bottle at her feet and neat whiskey in her stomach. I sat down in a chair near her bed. I'd been in her room only once since we arrived, to make sure it was comfortable for her. It was like her secret inner self; she invited no one in, and one came to respect it as inviolate. Yet there was nothing to see. Neat as a pin, it disclosed nothing of a personal nature, not a photograph or book. She even stowed away her needlepoint. She kept her room in my house in California the same way, like a room in an institution or a convent school. She was like a Chinese box, secret within secret.

"Now then, Lilah, what was that all about? What were you doing there in that entryway?"

She turned her face away on her pillow and moaned, "I don't want to talk about it."

"You must. We must have it out now."

"I was watching for your car from the upstairs window. I was upset. I saw you drive in and I went out to meet you and then I couldn't find you."

"What were you upset about?"

"I don't want to talk about it."

Almost at the end of my patience, I tried to speak gently and kindly. "Tell me, please, Lilah."

She kept silent.

"Did you have a row with Colin?"

Great tears promptly rolled down her cheeks.

"All right, what happened?"

She shook her head. "I can't repeat it." Her speech was thickening. I had made her a little drunk.

"Did he say something to upset you?"

"Sue, I want to go home!" Her chin puckered and fresh tears fell.

"We're leaving Monday."

"I don't want to wait till Monday. I want to leave tomorrow. As soon as Dottie gets home."

I stiffened. "How do you know Dottie's coming home tomorrow?"

"We stopped at the hoth – *hos*pital on our way back from Inverness. Oh, Sue, we'd had such a nice time, all day, laughing every minute! And we though we'd th – *stop*, and pay Dottie a little visit, only it was after visiting hours and the nurse told us she was coming home tomorrow anyway, and we left."

"Was this after your falling-out with Colin?"

"No, before. It was on the road between Kirkangus and the castle that it happened. Oh Sue!" She warbled off into sobs again.

I sat with my arms folded while she wept. My nerves, I discovered, were vibrating from head to foot. There had been enough excitement for one day. I had no idea what time it was. I felt as if the encounter with Hugh, underground in the castle, had been a fantasy, the strength and security of his arms as we stood beside the open drop, a bizarre dream.

Lilah had quieted, her eyes closed. She breathed evenly and deeply.

I struggled to my feet, lame again, bruised, close to the limit of exhaustion. I spread an extra quilt over her. "Lilah," I said, "I'm going to leave you now, but I'll be in my room. We'll talk in the morning. Don't make any decisions until then. I'll have some hot soup sent up to you if you like."

I don't think she heard me. She was already half-asleep.

I said softly, bending over her, "Lilah, was it you, following me in those underground passages?"

Her lips parted and she snored. I still couldn't be sure she wasn't faking.

IV. . . .

"Are you all right, Sue-love? Did you have any dinner? I brought you a wee dram."

Colin's cheerful unlined face, his mischievous black eyes, have become welcome to me, but at the moment I didn't think I could stand another confrontation.

"Jean sent my supper up." I was in my robe, ready for bed. I leaned my head against the doorjamb for a second and then straightened, stifling a groan. "Come in, Colin. Thank you for the drink. I'll use it as a nightcap." I took the glass from him and he came in and I closed the door.

I went to perch on my bed and Colin draped himself as comfortably as possible on the mad wood-carver's entry in Queen Victoria's Throne Contest.

"Colin, what did you say to Lilah?"

"Oh Lord. She took it to heart then."

"She certainly did."

He crossed his knees and breathed a puff through nearly closed lips. He swung his free foot. "You don't think she protested too much?"

"I don't know." I sipped my drink. "I wondered."

His eyebrows drew up ruefully. "We had a nice day, really we did. Lots of laughs. I *know* she enjoyed herself."

"Stop beating around the bush, Colin. Your ungoverned tongue has finally got you into trouble." I hadn't expected him to cheer me up, or wanted him to, but that is what his presence was doing. "What happened?"

"Well, we stopped at the hospital in Kirkangus to see Dottie but got turned away, and then Lilah asked to drive the rest of the way home. It gave me a small peculiar feeling, because I couldn't see why she wanted to, but I decided not to make an issue of it, and I said Sure, and she took over. And everything went fine, we bowled along quite correctly, except all of a sudden she was very quiet. Was she tired, or was there something about the hospital that gave her food for thought? I was scared suddenly. It was that quietness we talked about last night. She seemed about to — to spring! Susan, she was the Lilah who scares me!"

"Go on."

"We were heading down that steep drop with all the sharp curves that leads to the loch, and I thought to myself, She's going to pull something, I don't know what or how, but she's up to something, and I said, 'Easy does it, now, Lilah, we don't want to go off the road,' and she flared up, she got red in the face. I must have hit a nerve. She said, 'I'm much too good a driver to go off the road!' " He fell silent.

"Colin, go on, go on."

He made a grimace, a resigned sort of Charlie Brown face. "Oh, hell, Sue, I said the first thing that came into my head. Yes, my ungovernable tongue again! I said, 'You're too good a driver to get in the same car with someone who's going off the road —' "

"Colin!"

"I know, it was inexcusable, and I told her I was sorry and I was only kidding, but the damage was done. Damn it, Susan, I *am* sorry. I must have been a lot more uptight than I realized. And yet, and yet, maybe it's not a bad idea that she knows *somebody* has made a wild guess!"

I shut my eyes. "Oh Colin. I'll be glad when this is over. Lilah wants to leave. I don't know whether to go, too, or wait until Monday, or crawl under the bedclothes and stay there."

"Crawl under the bedclothes," he advised,

and bounced to his feet, impenitent as ever, relieved perhaps, like a guilty child who discovers he's not going to be punished after all. "Don't worry, love, I'll make it up to Lilah, you'll see. I must get some sleep, we're going out before dawn." He yawned. "I may be an idiot to try it, I'm certainly not in the peak of condition, like your gorgeous laird, but I can't resist an opportunity to tell my chums in Burbank I went deer stalking in Scotland. Bart and Andrew used to take me hunting in the Rockies and I loved it."

"Will you have to be out all day, Colin? Maybe you should call it quits halfway, at lunchtime, before you overtire yourself."

"That might be frowned upon, especially by the laird. I never let on to Bart and Andrew I was tired." He turned to me at the door. "But I'll gladly come back if you want me to, in fact, I don't have to go at all if you −"

"No, no, I'll be all right. I'm to fetch Dottie at noon."

"Okay, darling. Bolt your door. Then crawl under the covers. Ta, love!" And he was gone.

A strange noise woke me in the night, a rattling not on my door but on my window, the one facing the loch. I rose up in bed. It was sleet. The rain has changed to sleet, and an icy wind hurled it against the panes, making the sheer white curtains writhe like frantic ghosts. Poor Colin! But if the storm hasn't stopped by morning he surely won't go out in it.

"Something could happen to Colin, too, that could never be explained . . ."

That brought me wide awake. I've begun to react with anger at these remembered hints. I would settle for almost anything, short of my own death, to be free of them.

I turned on my light, wrapped a woolen throw around my shoulders, and took up my journal, which I'd put aside half-finished earlier.

Will this be my witness, this journal? Or will my executioner, knowing of its existence, hunt it out and destroy it? The minutes tick away, and I have no more doubt, since talking with Colin, that before noon tomorrow when I go to fetch Dottie, time will have run out, and I will either live to report it or the journal will come to an end with this entry.

Suspicion produces only chaos, not confirmation. My wanting this horror to end makes me prepare for it, and perhaps it is my readiness that makes me sure the end is coming.

Now, after writing for an hour, completing the report of the day, the wind has dropped and there is a subtle silence — not just the hush of the sleeping castle but the breath-held kind that follows a storm. I get out of bed and go to the window. I look down on a spectral scene — castle, loch, hills, bathed in moonlight, shrouded in snow. The sleet changed to snow before the storm ended. Clouds race across the moon, and the light fades as I stand in the icy air.

I hurry back to bed. Perhaps now, like a person stupefied by pain, or exhaustion, or the fulfillment of lovemaking, I will slide down into the pit of sleep. Perhaps, remembering Hugh's arms holding me, I will read his message, and dream, at least, of happiness.

CHAPTER 15

I. . . .

I slept until after nine and awoke to the white world. It was still freezing and the sky was overcast, and I thought of the Hebridean Islands and the tossing seas and the desolate world to the west in the path of the storm. The reflected whiteness filled my room, and for a moment I felt the childhood wonder I'd known in my native state of Washington – the womblike sense of safety, the pure joy.

But childhood was long gone and today there was no safety for me, or wonder, or joy.

I said one of my blind wordless prayers, not daring to believe, not daring to disbelieve: Let me just get through the next few hours until Dottie comes!

So I was dependent on her, for my very life, and there was no way out of it.

Again Chrissie brought me a note from Colin.

Sue-love, Jesus God what weather, I must be

*mad to go out on such a day. I'm going to quit at
noon as you suggested and the hell with His
Lordship's scorn. Can you pick me up on your
way to get Dottie? Dougal says we're going to try
the hills north of the loch. We'll go off in the Land
Rover but I'll walk back to the loch. Can you meet
me at the far end? I want to photograph the view
of the castle from there, it's breathtaking, in the
snow it should be pure Japanese. Hell, darling, the
truth is I'm concerned about you and want to be at
your side. Your loving, Colin.*

I was dressing when the timid knock I'd been
half-expecting, half-dreading, came at my door.

"Am I disturbing you?" Lilah queried.
"Chrissie told me you were up."

"You're not disturbing me." I didn't trust
myself to look at her. "How are you feeling?"

"My goodness, I slept like a dog. Did you
give me a sleeping pill? I don't remember."

"I gave you a stiff slug of Scotch."

"Oh." She didn't sit down but hovered about,
opening and shutting the clasp of her big
purse. "I guess it was called for. I'm sorry,
Susan —"

"Lilah, no apologies, no explanations, please.
I haven't time."

"You're going out?"

"Yes, I'm going to the hospital for Dottie."

"May I come with you?"

268

I spun about. "Why, Lilah? Why do you want to come with me?"

She answered deliberately. "Because I don't want to be alone. Because I don't want you to be alone. Because I want to talk to you."

"I'm not sure I want to talk now, Lilah. I don't think there's much point. And besides, I'm picking Colin up on my way to Kirkangus."

"Then I *must* talk to you, Susan," she said quietly, imploringly. "Susan, if you never do another thing for me, please take me with you now!"

So be it, I thought, standing empty-handed before my wardrobe mirror.

I wanted the end, and maybe this is it, I thought. Colin is away, Dottie isn't here yet, I'm alone; the stage is set. I felt thin suddenly in this moment of decision, as if my body had shrunk, as if there wasn't much of me left to kill. I wondered at myself: did I really not care any more, at the same time that I'd come to love life? Or was I indeed standing on my own two feet? Perhaps courage meant turning and meeting fate. Perhaps I wasn't really afraid of Lilah. Perhaps deep within me, where dead prayers repose, there was more belief than disbelief.

"All right, Lilah. I'll meet you downstairs in half an hour. I must attend to some things first."

She moved to the door. She, too, seemed to

have come to the bottom line. "I'll be there," she said quietly, and left.

I paid my bill at the desk. Lilah's too, and Dottie's. "I'll take care of the balance Monday," I told Jean, "but I'd like to get caught up now in case I need to stop at the bank in Kirkangus."

Jean said, embarrassed, "I don't know if you expected – if your brother-in-law was correct in assuming –"

"Of course." I had to smile. I paid Colin's bill, too.

"Jean," I said, "would you put this in the safe for me?" I gave her my journal.

"Certainly." She looked at me sharply. My face may have disturbed her. "It will be good to have Mrs. O'Halloran back with us," she said hopefully.

"Yes, it will."

"Be careful on the road. The snow is melting but there may be slippery patches."

"I'll be careful."

"Susan –" She didn't know what to say, she didn't know what was the matter.

"Yes, Jean." I looked her in the eye. "Don't worry."

I turned from her anxious face to find Lady Fanquill beside me. She put out her hand. She wanted to detain me also.

I drew back the fur collar of my coat to show the dress under it. "I have a talisman, you see," I told them both, "and it has already proved itself."

Then Lilah was approaching soundlessly over the carpet. I fell in with her, and without a word we went out the door together.

II. . . .

I drove. I wasn't going to go so far as to give Lilah the wheel. But as soon as we crossed the bridge I said, "All right, Lilah. What is it you want to tell me?"

"I'm hoping you can tell yourself, Sue." Her voice sounded faraway and tired. I couldn't get used to this genuinely subdued Lilah. I wondered if she had a hangover. She said, "You still don't remember much about the day of the accident in California, do you?"

"I remember the accident and that's enough," I told her. Involuntarily a forgotten fury colored my voice.

But she didn't seem to notice. "I mean what preceded the accident."

I took my eyes off the road long enough to turn my face to her. "I remember you were there for lunch."

"Yes," she said in her monotone. "Anything else? Anyone else?"

I stared ahead. For the first time, clear and plain as a perfectly focused color photograph, I saw the brick-paved patio where we usually lunched, the clay pots of geraniums and begonias, I saw the table set with Mexican mats, I saw Bart at the head of it, Lilah on his right and myself on his left and — at the end of the table, who? Somebody else . . .

I put my hand over my mouth. I swallowed. "Colin," I said faintly. "Colin was there too."

"Yes, Colin was there."

Was that what she wanted me to tell myself? But Colin said he hadn't seen much of us before the accident, he was busy on special effects for "Cops."

I went on remembering out loud, as though now I'd started I couldn't stop. The archaeologist's find was coming into view. "After lunch we sat around the pool . . . and that's when Bart . . . announced I was pregnant. Everyone was delighted. Then Colin left . . ."

And the garage was behind and below the house, out of sight of everyone but the servants, who were off that day because it was Sunday . . . And Colin, whose special-effects job was a television series full of car chases and spectacular smash-ups, had to have some mechanical know-how . . .

My head ached. My forehead felt red and swollen.

"Susan," said Lilah quietly, "he was also with Andrew the day he died."

I started. Was it possible to react to one more shock? "But —"

"He dropped in," Lilah continued. "It was when we had the old house on Eldorado Street. I left the two brothers to visit by themselves in the back yard, because Colin didn't drop in often, and I went upstairs to get on with some sewing. I looked out the back window finally because it was getting late, and I saw that Colin had gone and Andrew was — I thought at first — asleep in his deck chair."

I waited, scarcely breathing.

"Well, I don't know," she said. "I've never known. It was his heart, of course, and I'd prepared myself as much as one can for a final attack. But the doctor said he'd been dead a couple of hours! I thought then that he must have had the attack right after Colin left, because Colin told me Andrew was perfectly fine when they said good-bye. But after Bart's death . . . I couldn't help wondering if perhaps Andrew'd had the attack *before* Colin left, and Colin went away without calling me, *left* him, *knowing* —" She had begun to raise her voice and she broke off again. "I couldn't help won-

dering if that started him off, eliminating everyone in his way!"

She cleared her throat. "And yesterday he as
good as implied I was responsible for both
Andrew's and Bart's deaths! That's what upset
me so! To think I would let my own husband
die! And murder Bart, who'd been so good to
me, and you, and your baby – !" Her voice
threatened to rise into a scream, but she caught
herself again and coughed.

"And one more thing, Susan. Colin knew
Dottie had headaches because I told him, his
first morning here. I said, 'The only time I ever
have Susan to myself is when Dottie goes off to
take her aspirin and lie down.' Oh, God, Sue,
I'm a born blunderer, I've blundered all along,
casting aspersions on Dottie, taking you out in
that boat . . ."

I made one final grasp at sanity. "Lilah, both
you and Colin could be mistaken! They could
have been natural deaths. The police investi-
gated the car accident; *they* couldn't find
evidence of homicide, and they must have
looked for it as a matter of routine."

"They couldn't find *proof*, maybe. Sue, I've
tried to believe it wasn't homicide myself, even
after Colin followed you here, even after Dottie
had to be removed to the hospital, even after he
insisted on visiting the hospital yesterday and

274

found out when she was coming home!" Lilah was wringing her hands. "But last night I stopped trying. Listen, Sue. Let me tell you about it. Last night I *knew* Colin was up to something."

III. . . .

We were halfway down the loch-road with its whitened verges. I was puttering along more and more slowly, and now I pulled over to the side of the road and sat there, staring ahead, my vision blinking in time with my throbbing skull.

Lilah hurried now. "Colin dropped me at the main door when we got home from Inverness, and drove off in the rain to put the car away." Her voice stumbled a little over the words. "I went upstairs but I was so upset by what he'd said to me that I went first to your door. I wanted to blurt it all out to you. Then when I found you hadn't got back from Kirkangus I went to the window in the upstairs hall to watch for you, with all those terrible thoughts going through my head about Andrew, and Bart, and *you* . . ."

I imagined her standing there wringing her hands, as she was doing now.

"And finally I saw your car coming across the causeway. It was getting dark. And at the same moment I wondered, I don't know why, *Where's Colin?* Did he come back from the garage? Is he still *there*, waiting for Sue? My mind painted terrible pictures of him forcing you to breathe carbon monoxide from the exhaust of your car, making it look like another accident, or suicide . . . I ran and knocked on his door and there was no answer, and I didn't waste any more time looking for him, I ran down the back stairs to the drive. By that time you had already reached the garage, and I ran on, and when I got there you'd left your car and gone. But I saw *him!*"

I had brought my hands together at the bottom of the steering wheel, close to my chest. I ached all over as I used to in the hospital months ago.

"He was going through the archway that leads from the garage to the — what is it, a stable? Susan, I didn't like the way he *moved*, hurrying, bent over, running close to the shadow of the wall, skulking! I ran after him, not making any noise on my rubber soles in the teeming rain. I went through the arch and thought I'd lost him, but I saw the door ajar at the end of the yard. And then, as I headed for it Lord Greggan came out of one of the stalls and went in the door ahead of me." Lilah buried her face in her hands. "I got as far as the entry but I was too cowardly to go further, I was afraid of getting lost, it was so dark in there —" She was babbling.

I grasped her arm. "All right, Lilah, all right!" I started the car again, and we passed the fork in the road where one branch goes up the hill to Kirkangus and the other to the end of the loch.

My brain was incapable of figuring anything out any more. Everything I'd suspected of Lilah could in fact be suspected of Colin. I realized my fondness of Colin didn't include complete trust, never had. I could picture his glistening dark eyes and knew he, too, had his secret inner world, and that an unfathomable intelligence lay behind those eyes.

"Lilah, was it you in the window the other night, when Colin and I got home from the *ceilidh*?"

"So you saw me," she sighed. "Well, I don't care. I've been worried about you a long time, wondering about Colin. I couldn't sleep. I knew Jean and Jock had come in, I heard them having a terrible argument in the bar, but I couldn't locate *you*. And then at that same window I spotted you and Colin on the bridge. Sue, I only wanted to make sure you got in safely!"

"Yes. All right." I was sick and exhausted and fed up and empty of all but despair. "Lilah,

277

after I pick Colin up I'm going to take you both back to the castle. After this session I don't think I could bear —"

"I think it would be wise. But, Susan, until you drop us both off I'm not leaving your side!"

I drew up at the end of the loch beside a little fringe of fir trees. I sounded the horn once, to let Colin know we were there. "You said last night you wanted to leave today, Lilah, after Dottie comes back from the hospital. Do you still want to go?'

The tears began to run down her face. "Yes. As long as you're not alone. But, Susan, I want you to know I love you and am grateful for all —"

I turned away to the window, shaking my head. "Oh, Lilah, no, please!" If Dottie and Colin were right about her, then her words now were abominable.

She persisted, staring at the dashboard. "I want you to be happy more than I want to be happy myself. I think you've suffered more and deserve happiness more."

I didn't know how to answer her. I had no responses left. I wished Colin would come. I needed air.

I said, "Let's not talk about it any more. I'm going to get out and look back at the castle. Colin says it's a breathtaking view. He may be photographing it." I wanted to go by myself but I knew she would stick to me. I had a strange feeling of going through preordained motions, like an automaton, of moving helplessly according to plan.

So we got out of the car together and threaded our way through the firs bordering the water, with the barren wall of Craggy Head looming up to our left. A mist rose from the melting snow, transforming the vague sunlight to mother-of-pearl.

It wouldn't have been hard for Colin to guess my feelings for Hugh Greggan, confused though they might be, and he knew I wouldn't want to miss seeing Hugh's castle from a matchless vantage point. And Colin was right; there it was at the far end of the loch, the turreted pile etched in white, mirrored in the still water, rising out of the low mist, so that both castle and reflection seemed to float. It was indeed like a Japanese print, its colors muted, cool and mysterious.

The powdered branches around us gave off a piney fragrance and I lifted my face to it, my breath rising in frosty plumes, and tried to shed torment, drinking in the chill misted air, the atmosphere of moral certainty and purity.

I shouldn't have closed my eyes. In the next instant Lilah gave me a violent shove, and simultaneously with the rifle crack I fell forward on my knees. I had no cane to support me.

Immediately there was another shot, and then a third, the hills tossing the explosions back and forth, and as I raised my head I saw the body fall, and the gun, both of them cartwheeling in midair, down the sheer face of Craggy Head. "Colin − !" I covered my ears against the sound of his body hitting the ground.

I moved in slow motion, picking myself up. Lilah was lying on her back behind me, the light fading from her eyes, the tiny lines at the corners of her mouth saying, Isn't this ridiculous? There was a reddening spot on her gabardine coat, over her heart.

I heard someone making terrible noises, a sobbing that was almost retching, and never knew it was myself.

When Hugh reached me, his gun still under his arm, I let myself go, face down in the snow beside Lilah.

He knelt and lifted me up. "Susan, Susan, are you hurt?"

I couldn't speak. I shook my head.

Clever Colin, arranging everything, waiting for me on Craggy Head! He could have claimed he mistook me for a deer in my tan coat and fur collar, half-obscured in the mist.

But he hadn't counted on Lilah coming with

me. Lilah must have spotted him taking aim, at the top of the ledge, and having shoved me down, she received the first bullet. I'll never know if it was meant for me or Lilah, or if the second bullet was meant for the one of us who was left. My guess is that he aimed for me twice, and missed, and would have gone on shooting until he killed me. He had won his sharpshooter's medal too long ago.

The third bullet, which didn't miss, was Hugh's. Colin had been culled from the herd.

"Your shadow is gone," Hugh told me, rocking me, his cheek against mine.

CHAPTER 16

I. . . .

I did go back to the Place of Peace after all,
before we left Strathburne.

The police formalities were over, the inquiry
completed by that uniquely Scottish official,
the Procurator Fiscal, or the Fiscal for short.
Due to the extenuating circumstances of the
shootings on Craggy Head, it was doubtful that
the case would ever come to trial. There was too
much weight on Hugh's side and too much
evidence of the crimes of Colin MacLarkie.
Nevertheless Mr. Thornhill conducted an im-
partial service in a thundering no-nonsense
voice over the ashes of Lilah and Colin before
they were sent back to the States, and his
powerful invocations, consigning their souls to
almighty justice, helped to clear the air. The
tears I shed for them after that fell only late at
night, when I was alone.

Two weeks had passed when Dottie and I at
last packed our bags ("By Jesus, kiddo, if I ever

leave home again it will be with my own policeman!"), and only a day remained before we left for Glasgow.

Then Hugh's note arrived. Would I give him an hour that afternoon? I wrote a reply asking if he would take me out to my estate once more.

We had become a sort of family in these two weeks. Wilbur Grant and the Barsington-Bankses had departed hurriedly the day after the tragedy — the major giving me a squeeze and a wink and a final "Rum!" before Mrs. Barsington-Banks hauled him away. An unexpected relaxation descended on those of us who were left, a quietness of spirit, free of anxiety but chastened. Or perhaps this was only my own inevitable reaction after the strain of the previous weeks. I had all the rest of my life now to sort out my feelings and put them to rest.

Between solemn duties I took long walks with Jean, aided by my cane, which Hugh had found for me as he had promised; and it was Jean's unspoken sympathy and bright, realistic approach to life which reinforced my growing acceptance. Hugh offered me the use of his library on the top floor of his tower while he was away in the hills with Dougal, and saw to it that the paneled room was warmed with a hearth fire. His reading interests were broader than mine but I found comfort among his books, high in his isolated eyrie, and I felt I knew him better.

Dottie worked on her dazzling afghan in the lounge with Lady Fanquill, who made no move to leave for Edinburgh until our troubles were over. The hotel was officially closed and the staff reduced, and Gordon was everywhere at once, but he found time to take us on a sightseeing drive, ending up with tea at the manse with his turbulent father and unflappable mother. He invited us into the castle kitchen one afternoon for a lesson in making rumbledethump.

Every night we all sat down to dinner together, either in the castle dining room or the Greggans' cozy apartment. There were still pauses when the events of the past weeks struck us dumb, but once we got over feeling guilty about laughing we laughed a great deal. Hugh joined in the badinage with an effortless wit but he was still under some restraint and the haunted look had never left his eyes. They rested on me in passing for a second or two but we exchanged no private words at any time. Severn sat half-asleep with his eyes open, for he was up and out at dawn with the stalkers. One night, holding Jean's hand, Gordon sang for us.

Lady Fanquill was dozing alone by the fire as

I crossed the lounge for my final meeting with Hugh.

"You do not need a talisman any longer, do you?" she asked, opening her eyes.

I halted; my hand went to my lapel. "You want it back, Lady Fanquill?"

"I want you to keep it forever. But since you are no longer in danger you can now begin to trust people, can you not?"

I went over and perched beside her. "You mean, don't you, that you'd like me to trust your nephew?"

She smiled, her vague aquamarine eyes searching my face. "You are knowing, are you not? I have always been aware we had intuitiveness in common. Yes, I would like you now to trust Hugh Greggan. Once, before these tragedies, he had the power to hurt you, not only because he could be hurtful in his own way but because you could be vulnerable in yours. It is the last thing in the world he would wish to do today."

"He never wished to," I said quietly, taking her hand in mine and studying its fairylike frailty. "And I have always trusted him. The question is, can he trust me?"

"No, my dear." She shook her head. "Perhaps after all the question is, can you trust yourself?"

285

She closed her eyes and dozed off again.

It was mild as May, one of those radical changes in weather the British Isles are noted for. The snow had long ago melted away. The October sky was absolutely cloudless, the sun warm. We sat as before on Hugh's plaid, the air stirring gently around us, the animated stillness quieting us, the moors and hills rolling out before us.

Hugh still didn't know the land would return to Strathburne after I left. Archibald MacBaine had honored my request for silence.

And now in this lonely beauty, close to Hugh, I felt a terrible heaviness of heart, and wondered at myself for wanting to come here. I felt the tears press suddenly behind my eyes like the accumulated weight of a flood against a dam. The prospect ahead of me in California was not a happy one. For the first time I was going to be entirely alone, and I must begin life over again. I knew that I would remember this moment with longing, and think of these hills as if they had been my home.

"So it's good-bye then," Hugh said.

"Yes." I didn't trust myself to say more. As if gauged to the ounce of pressure, the dam broke and the tears rolled out, silently coursing down

286

my cheeks and spilling on my jacket.

He sat as before, clasping his knees, looking ahead at the view. He said, "I want you to know this. I've never killed a man. It does not rest lightly on my conscience. When he left us in the hills at noon to join you, I knew from his walk it was he who had followed you underground in the castle the night before, knew what it was that troubled you, guessed at the atrocities he'd already perpetrated. There is no mistaking the walk and bearing of a stalker, and I stalked him in turn. I thought, You shall not harm that lovely gentle woman, and I knew what I felt for you and that I would kill for you."

"But you had to take his life to save mine, the Fiscal himself conceded that." I mopped my face with my sleeve, thankful he wasn't looking at me. "Hugh, you mustn't feel guilty."

He reached for my hand. "Only you, Susan — not the Fiscal, not Thornhill the minister, no one but you, could tell me that and absolve me." He seemed to hold his breath for an instant. Then he said quickly in a low voice, still without looking at me, "Susan, I want never to part with you, I want to discover life with you." He turned to me at last as if in anger, eyes deepened in color, hand gripping painfully. "I can't bear to say good-bye to you."

I looked back at him. My lips parted to speak.

"No," he said. "Better I finish. I brought you here to lay it out before you, not to make you answer, for I know you must go home. Susan, something in that act on Craggy Head made me yours absolutely, united me with you like the act of love. And yet it makes no claim on you, you are as free of me as the day you arrived, and probably, given time, I can find it in myself to wish you well without me."

He looked suddenly away to the view but kept my hand. The light breeze stirred his flaxen hair. "But from the very first, when I looked into your half-drowned face, I've loved you, wanted you shamelessly, tormentingly. I want you now, this moment."

He drew in another long breath, let it out. He turned to me, half-smiling as if in despair at himself. He said quietly, "Susan Burns, I do ask. I ask in spite of everything. I ask you to come back to me."

I looked confidently, amazedly, into his eyes. The ragged bits and pieces of my life were coming together, doubt was turning into certainty, confusion resolving into order. It had begun with relinquishing him, standing alone and facing danger, accepting the harsh and the benign. Before that I'd never had strength of my own with which to meet strength, or passion of my own with which to share passion.

288

It wasn't even necessary to think this through, for I'd learned something else, that I did indeed trust myself.

He said, "I wouldn't expect you to bury yourself in the Highlands with me. In winter we could see a little of the world . . ."

"A palazzo in Venice," I murmured, "a casbah in Marrakesh, a houseboat in Kashmir . . ." For a long time, probably, Colin's whimsical remarks would come back to me.

But Hugh said calmly, "Aye, why not? There is unlimited territory to explore, unknown to us because we have never explored it together; all the wonders, all the ecstasies. Are you shy of venturing into the unknown?"

"Not any more, Hugh."

"No more am I. I ask you to explore it with me, Susan. I ask you to be my wife."

I want you to be happy more than I want to be happy myself. They were Lilah's last words to me, and I owed it to her never to forget them.

I said, "Would we be married in the chapel?"

A quick smile indented his cheeks with the vertical dimples.

"That is what I had in mind."

"Would Mr. Thornhill marry us?"

"He would leap at the chance, as only Mr. Thornhill can leap."

"Would I wear a ruby-red dress like a crusader's lady?"

"Aye, with a little bridal crown of gold and pearls, worn in the Fourteenth century by a Strathburne lady. And never, I might add, worn since." Considerately, he wanted me to know Gwendolyn hadn't worn it.

"Would Jean attend me?"

"That is what *she* has in mind. I daresay she chose you for my wife even before I did. She might allow Gordon to give you away. Severn will want to bear something, a ring or a train or a banner, whatever needs bearing. Munro will throw open doors."

"And Lady Fanquill?"

"She will smile as if she foresaw it all from the beginning."

"I have no doubt she did. May I invite Dottie and her husband? And Mrs. Kenzie MacLarkie?"

"If I may invite some eccentric chiefs of clans and a handful of very odd-looking scholars. There would have to be a feast in the great hall afterward, of course, with pipers."

"Of course." I smiled. I leaned forward and kissed him slowly and softly and firmly on the lips, as he had kissed me, in the depths of the castle. He seemed to stop breathing.

"That is my message to you, Hugh. I have

290

wanted you from the start, and that's all I thought it was, a physical wanting; but when I let go of it, to spare us both from further torment, I found I wanted never to leave you. I love you with all my heart. I want to discover life with you. I will come back to you."

For a long time we held each other, not kissing.

He drew back slowly, and as his eyes searched mine, time seemed to stop again and everything hung in the balance. The sounds of infinitesimal life around us, the faint rustlings and cracklings, became clamorous, the sun-warmed fragrances of earth and grass intoxicating. And I felt, perhaps like Lady Fanquill, that in this timelessness, in a place of peace, where history was all one, Hugh and I were already united.

"Yes," I breathed, for peace is affirmative, and there was nothing left, now, but Yes.

THORNDIKE PRESS HOPES you have enjoyed this Large Print book. All our Large Print titles are designed for the easiest reading, and all our books are made to last. Other Thorndike Press Large Print books are available at your library, through selected bookstores, or directly from the publisher. For more information about current and upcoming titles, please call us, toll free, at 1-800-223-6121, or mail your name and address to:

THORNDIKE PRESS
P. O. BOX 159
THORNDIKE, MAINE 04986

There is no obligation, of course.

DATE DU